Jeremy Strong once worked in a bakery, putting the jam into three thousand doughnuts every night. Now he puts the jam in stories instead, which he finds much more exciting. At the age of three, he fell out of a first-floor bedroom window and landed on his head. His mother says that this damaged him for the rest of his life and refuses to take any responsibility. He loves writing stories because he says it is 'the only time you alone have complete control and can make anything happen'. His ambition is to make you laugh (or at least snuffle). Jeremy Strong lives near Bath with four cats and a flying cow.

Are you feeling silly enough to read more?

LAUGH YOUR SOCKS OFF WITH

Jeremy STRONG

Krazy Kow

Saves the World

- Well, Almost

Illustrated by

Nick Sharratt

PUFFIN

PUFFIN BOOKS

Published by the Penguin Group
Penguin Books Ltd, 80 Strand, London WC2R ORL, England
Penguin Group (USA) Inc., 375 Hudson Street, New York, New York 10014, USA
Penguin Group (Canada), 90 Eglinton Avenue East, Suite 700, Toronto, Ontario, Canada M4P 2Y3
(a division of Pearson Penguin Canada Inc.)
Penguin Ireland, 25 St Stephen's Green, Dublin 2, Ireland (a division of Penguin Books Ltd)
Penguin Group (Australia), 250 Camberwell Road, Camberwell, Victoria 3124, Australia
(a division of Pearson Australia Group Pty Ltd)
Penguin Books India Pvt Ltd, 11 Community Centre, Panchsheel Park, New Delhi – 110 017, India
Penguin Group (NZ), 67 Apollo Drive, Mairangi Bay, Auckland 1310, New Zealand
(a division of Pearson New Zealand Ltd)
Penguin Books (South Africa) (Pty) Ltd, 24 Sturdee Avenue, Rosebank, Johannesburg 2196, South Africa

Penguin Books Ltd, Registered Offices: 80 Strand, London WC2R ORL, England

penguin.com

First published 2002
This edition published 2007

15

Text copyright © Jeremy Strong, 2002
Illustrations copyright © Nick Sharratt, 2002
All rights reserved

The moral right of the author and illustrator has been asserted

Set in Baskerville MT
Made and printed in England by Clays Ltd, St Ives plc

British Library Cataloguing in Publication Data
A CIP catalogue record for this book is available from the British Library

ISBN: 978-0-141-32239-1

www.greenpenguin.co.uk

MIX
Paper from
responsible sources
FSC® C018179
www.fsc.org

This is for my pal Hal.
And I would also like to
thank Yvonne H. for wrestling with Time
Frames and a recalcitrant author and for being
Seriously Cool at all times.

Contents

1 How I Gave Birth to a Cow

I'm going to be famous. My name will be known all over the world. People will say: 'Look! There's Jamie Frink! I've met Jamie Frink! Let's ask him for his autograph!'

And I'll say, 'Yeah, sure, have three!'

You'll see. Everyone will see, even my Big Bro.

Yeah, that'll show him. He thinks he's so clever, but when I'm rich and famous he'll look like a widdly-weeny ant next to me. He'll be nothing.

When he wants something, he'll have to come to me. And I'll say, 'Hmmm, maybe.'

And you know what's going to make me rich and famous? A cow. Yeah, a cow.

Her name is Krazy Kow. This is what she looks like.

She's fantastic, Krazy Kow. She's got a lumpy head, a lumpy back and wobbly lumps underneath. She can talk too, and she's got a Swiss  army udder. She has, really! You know what a Swiss army penknife is like, with lots of gadgets? Well, Krazy Kow's udder doesn't just squirt milk. She also has a flame-thrower, rocket launcher, water cannon, high-beam spotlight, mega-powerful vacuum cleaner and mirror for checking her make-up. (Plus a small prongy thing for getting stones out of horses' hoofs.)

She's got four stomachs too, and that means she can do four separate burps, all at the same time and on different notes. (Did you know cows have four stomachs? It's true. I'm not kidding.) And she can do karate. Just in case things get close and personal.

Krazy Kow lives in a house with Mr and Mrs Spottiswood and their two children, a boy called Bromley and a girl called Gosforth.

Bromley has got football wallpaper all over his bedroom walls and a United duvet cover and a lampshade like a football. Actually his head's a bit like a football too – nothing in it but air.

Gosforth's bedroom is full of pop stars. Not real ones, just photographs. Gosforth kisses every one of them before she goes to sleep at night.

Krazy Kow doesn't have a bedroom, because that would be REALLY SILLY. Everybody knows cows don't have bedrooms. Ha! No, she sleeps under the dining table. She curls up beneath the table, with her blanket and teddy.

Of course, she's not real. And the Spottiswood family isn't real either. I made them all up! They're cartoon characters, inside my head, rushing about.

I'm always sketching them. I've drawn cows everywhere, especially on my school books. My teachers think I've got cows on the brain, and I suppose that in an odd way they're right. I have.

I reckon Krazy Kow is going to be on TV one day, and then she'll be the most famous cow in the world. There'll be Krazy Kow T-shirts and everyone will want them. There'll be Krazy Kow mugs and everyone will drink from them. There'll be Krazy Kow duvet covers and everyone will

sleep under them – everyone except my Big Brother, but then he's stupid.

And best of all, everyone will do what Krazy Kow says, and because *I'm* telling her what to say, it means that everyone will be doing what I tell them. Awesome!

Of course, she'll only tell people good things,

because she's a good cow. Baddie cows are the pits. You can easily tell if a cow is bad because baddie cows always have plastic tags with numbers attached to their ears, which shows that they have been in cow prison for being bad.

Krazy Kow is good. In fact, she's a cow superhero and eco-warrior. She whizzes about preventing ecological disasters, Saving the World and stuff like that. Maybe she'll save Big Bro too. I don't know. Hmmm, maybe.

Now, perhaps you are beginning to think: This guy is mad. What is all this stuff about cows sleeping under tables and being put in cow prison for being bad?

I guess I'd better tell you how I thought up Krazy Kow, and why. At school we are taking part in a mega environmental competition. Schools right across the country are entering. The winning school gets a whole room full of computers. AND the winning project gets shown on TV. The person who comes up with the winning idea gets a digital video camera and film-editing system. We are talking Seriously Big Prizes here, and I was desperate to get my hands on that DV camera.

You see, all I've ever wanted to do is make REAL FILMS, with real actors and explosions and cars crashing down cliff sides, bounce, bounce, bang! And hurricanes and poisonous snakes and alien invaders with boiling green jelly for blood, and a nasty evil villain with one eye and steel teeth and claw hands, and giant crocodiles and volcanoes erupting living dinosaurs ... and all that sort of stuff.

Taking part in the environmental competition was Mrs Drew's idea. She's our head teacher. She's a great one for Saving the Planet. You should see her car. She's got this tiny little thing that she drives around. It does a million miles to a gallon of petrol, she says. In fact, I don't think it has an engine at all. I think that each tyre has got one of

those rotating hamster
wheels strapped to it and she
puts hamsters inside and
makes them run as fast as
possible. She's got a four-
hamster-powered car. I don't
know what she does if
they're asleep.

Anyway, the back window of Mrs Drew's car is
plastered with do-good stickers. You know the sort
of thing –

Mrs Drew is really kind to animals. It's just
children she doesn't like. No! I made that up. She
does like them really. I remember we were in
Assembly once and she told us that she had

always wanted to work with animals and that's why she became a teacher. I like Mrs Drew; she's a laugh.

Anyhow, Mrs Drew told us about this competition, and my ears perked up immediately. If there is one thing that a great film director needs, it's a camera so that he can shoot films, so I thought to myself: I've got to win this!

But winning the camera was not going to be easy. I knew that to have any chance of success I would have to do something VERY special, and first of all I would have to make sure that my idea was the one the school would choose.

I reckoned almost everyone would either write something about the environment, or they'd paint a poster. And that was when I had my first, absolutely staggering idea. I would make a film – a proper film! It would have to be the biggest secret ever, because I didn't want anybody else to get the same idea. I don't think anyone in our school had ever made a real film before.

I was so excited I had to tell someone. I had to say it out loud, so do you know what I did? I got inside my wardrobe. I pulled the door in close so that it wasn't quite shut, and I stood there in the dark, imagining I was in a room full of people

and I told the darkness how brilliant my idea to make a film was. (I realize this might sound strange but I like talking in the dark. You can say anything you want in the dark.)

And then someone knocked on the wardrobe.

It was Big Bro. (It would be.) I slowly pushed the door open and Matt gazed at me.

'What are you doing?'

I stood there among my clothes. 'Nothing.'

'You were talking to someone.'

'Oh yeah, like I've got someone in the wardrobe with me,' I said smartly.

'You're mad,' said Matt.

'So are you then,' I snapped back. (We have these really neat arguments sometimes.)

Matt snorted and pushed me back into the wardrobe. I tripped on a pile of trainers and sat down. The door swung to and clicked shut. I pushed against it and, sure enough, it wouldn't open.

'Matt, the door's shut.' There was no answer. 'Matt? Stop fooling. I know you're out there. Open the door. Matt? MATT!'

I clambered to my feet, still shouting. I hammered on the inside of the door and the wardrobe rocked unsteadily. I carried on shouting and hammering and all at once the wardrobe toppled forwards and slumped at an angle across my bed.

I ended up lying in a heap, completely entangled in clothes and wire coat hangers. I tried to get up and shake myself free but the noise was terrifying. It sounded like the Hundred-Legged Coat-Hanger Beast From Mars falling down the stairs.

I gave up. Everything went quiet. I settled back on the pile of clothes, in the dark, and it was surprisingly peaceful. I lay there thinking about the film I would make. The thing was, I needed a really good main character to fight ecological battles, someone like Superman, or Batman. Then I thought: Why not have a character that nobody would think of? Maybe not even a person. An alien? An animal …?

And that was when I had my second brainwave.

Oh yes! An animal! A Super Creature! By this time my brain was humming into sixth gear. This was fantastic!

There were footsteps outside. I called out. 'Hello? Is that you, Matt?'

'Jamie?' It was my big sister, Gemma. She's fourteen, but thinks she's at least nineteen. 'Where are you?'

'In the wardrobe.'

'How did you get in there?'

'Just help me out, will you?'

Gemma struggled to push the wardrobe upright. The door clicked open and I tumbled out, festooned with a clattering shower of coat hangers. Gemma looked mildly astonished.

(Which is quite easy for her because of the vast amount of dark make-up she splatters all over her face.) Behind her was Matt, laughing his head off. (I wish it *had* fallen off.)

Gemma helped me to my feet. 'What were you doing in there?'

'Thinking,' I answered.

'What about?'

I smiled at them both.

'A cow. A cow with a Swiss army udder.'

2 Reasons to be Cheerful/Miserable

Reasons to be Cheerful:
1. Can't think of any.
2. Oh yes, I'm going to be rich and famous.
3. That's the lot.

Reasons to be Miserable:
1. My dad likes football.
2. My mum likes football.
3. Big Bro is a football.
4. I don't like football.
5. They think I'm stupid. (I'm not.)

Anyhow, I've got news for everyone out there in the big, wide world. It's OK if you don't like football. That's right, it is NOT compulsory. Don't get me wrong. There's nothing wrong with football as a game. I don't mind watching football. I just don't like playing football. What gets me is

all those people who seem to think that BOYS
MUST LIKE PLAYING FOOTBALL.

Why? Don't ask me. The boys in my class are
mad about it. They've got favourite teams, even
though half of them keep changing their minds.
As soon as their team hits a losing streak they
change sides. So much for loyalty. And they go on
and on and on and on. Break time comes and off
they shoot to the playground. What shall we do?
Play footie!

Last week I suggested something else. I said
let's pretend we're making a film with loads of
special stunts and stuff. They stopped dead and
gawped at me like I was the Beast From the
Bubbling Bog. Then one of them said, I know,
let's play footie. Yeah! They all shouted. They're
so imaginative.

So I'm getting a bit fed up. I suppose that if I
was any good at footie I might enjoy it more, but

I'm hopeless. I'm the sort of person who takes a massive kick at the ball, completely misses and falls over backwards in the mud.

Not to worry. I'll show them. One day, when they're nobodies, they'll be watching one of my multi-Oscar-winning films on telly and they'll turn to their wives and their own little kids and they'll say: 'Wow! Do you see that? It says: Directed by Jamie Frink. I was at school with him.'

Big Bro and Dad are football freaks. They're always trying to get me to join in, but what's the point if all you do is fall flat on your back and bang your head so hard that all your teeth rattle and your ears fall off? I played with them at the weekend. They put me in goal and you know what? I don't think they were trying to get the ball in the net at all. They were just using me as target practice.

Bamm! The first shot spun me round like Wibbly Wobbly Man. Bamm! The second shot knocked my feet from

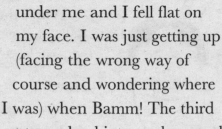

under me and I fell flat on my face. I was just getting up (facing the wrong way of course and wondering where I was) when Bamm! The third shot torpedoed into my bum and catapulted me into the net. I was left hanging there like a dead spider.

Sometimes I think they only want to play footie with me because I'm no good. After all, when I'm playing I make them look like geniuses. Mind you, Matt is pretty good. He's being eyed up for the county team. I just wish he wouldn't go on about it. Anyone would think he'd just been nominated for an Oscar.

There's something else I don't understand and it's this: the girls are just as bad. I'll swear most of them are not the least bit interested in football, but who do they all like? Who do they all fancy? Tom Hardy.

 Who's the best footballer in the school? Tom Hardy.

Who's team captain? Tom Hardy.

Who's Big Bro's best mate? Tom Hardy.

Who's got a brain like a bird dropping? Both of them.

You might have guessed that I don't like Tom much. It's not because he plays football so well. It's because of Rebecca. She's in our class. How can I describe her? Well, she's tall, long legs, suntanned, blonde, hazel eyes … Beautiful, I guess that's the best word. Forget anything else I said and just concentrate on beautiful. Maybe even stunning. She'd make a wonderful film star.

Rebecca's got a brain too. She writes fantastic stories. I mean, they're so good our teacher, Mr Oldman, reads them out to us. She uses really long words, like 'infatuated' and 'phantasmagoric'.

So, Rebecca is beautiful and bright. Does she speak to me? No. Does she speak to Tom Hardy? Yes. She even talks to my brother, for goodness' sake! She SMILES at them! I mean, they're not even in our class. They're a year older!

Anyhow, what does she see in Tom Hardy? All he does is kick a ball about very well. It's not much of a claim, is it? Look at me – I'm stuffed full of brilliant ideas. My stories are every bit as good as Rebecca's.

So maybe Mr Oldman doesn't read mine out, but that's because he doesn't understand them, doesn't appreciate them. The last story I wrote for him was about Krazy Kow. He pointed out that the title he had given the class was: MY WEEKEND.

'But that's what I did, Mr Oldman. I spent all weekend thinking about Krazy Kow.'

'Jamie, you were not supposed to write about what you were thinking, but about what you did. Did you do anything over the weekend?'

I nearly told him that I got a football up my backside, but stopped myself just in time.

'Your problem, Jamie, is that you live in a fantasy world.'

I nearly told him that fantasy was a lot better than the real world I lived in, but stopped myself just in time.

'You spend all day staring out of the window. You never do any work.'

I nearly told him that my head is working all the time, it's full of brilliant ideas, but stopped myself just in time.

'When are you going to write a proper story?'

I was stunned. I had spent all weekend writing the best story ever – you can see for yourself.

3 Krazy Kow's First Adventure

Scene One

Imagine a slug as big
as a wardrobe. Give
the slug a fat, fat face
and two chubby
arms. Now dress it in
a black suit, with
collar and tie. (The
trousers only have one
leg.) The front of the suit

is shiny with slime. The creature looks much like an
everyday businessman, except that he's very fat,
very slimy and basically a big slug, with arms.

You are looking at Gobb-Yobb Badmash, the Dark
Contaminator.

> *[Menacing music, like spooky footsteps*
>   *approaching:* **poom poom poom poom PAH!!!!]**

Gobb-Yobb Badmash slithers from his black

throne and slides forward to peer over the edge of
the Mappa Monstrosa, a living map of the entire
world, spread in a huge, flat circle, floating on a
sheen of shifting mercury, a deadly poison. The
Mappa Monstrosa is in some ways like a crystal ball,
in that you can look upon it and see what is
happening. Gobb-Yobb Badmash uses the Mappa to
watch his plans for world destruction slowly taking
place.

Hee hee hee, what a horrible villain he is, with his
plan to destroy the world, and his pockets full of
wriggling worms. Gobb-Yobb likes worms. He eats
them, like thin, slippery sweets. Shlurppp!

Bit by bit Gobb-Yobb is also eating away at the
Earth. Across Asia he has set fires that burn away
the last remaining forests. Sizzle, sizzle!

Across Europe he is poisoning
the land with pesticides, bringing
about the writhing agony of

SPISSS!

millions of insects, birds and beasts, through pesticide poisoning. Spissssss! Die, birdies! Die, beasties!

Across America he watches as people slowly foul their own air with the pollution of a billion car exhaust fumes, from their own cars. Brrrm, brrrm, cough, splutter, splutter, aaaaargh, THUMP!

BRRM BRRM!

[Sound effect: body falling down dead]

Gobb-Yobb gives a high-pitched giggle and turns to his sidekick, Secretary Snirch. 'People are so gweedy they don't even care if it means their own death,' he says.

'People are stupid, O Dark Contaminator,' agrees Secretary Snirch. 'What will you do today to add to their misery?'

Gobb-Yobb gazes down upon the Mappa Monstrosa and gives another high giggle. 'It's such a long time since we had a nuclear disaster, don't you think?'

'Such a long time,' sighs Secretary Snirch happily.

'I think, how about Austwalia? Let's do Austwalia! We'll cause such a mess. A little fire in a big weactor and, oh dear, there goes half the population!'

'And the radiation,' Secretary Snirch points out, 'it will spread.'

'It will! It will! How lovely! And we'll have a little huwwicane, just to stir things up a bit and move them along nicely. Oh, I am going to enjoy today. Pwepare the Chaos Computer, Snirch, and send down the Mashmen.'

Gobb-Yobb Badmash slithers back to his throne, closes his eyes and dreams of unnatural disasters, while a hundred Mashmen, in their black tights and polo-neck sweaters, advance, all creepily-sneakily, upon the doomed Australian nuclear reactor.

Scene Two

In the Spottiswood home, Krazy Kow is quietly doing a yoga handstand behind the sofa. Bromley is watching a football match on the television, leaping up and down on the sofa and yelling his head off.

'Come on, United! Give them grief! Foul! Kill the ref! Send in the troops!'

'You seem a trifle overexcited,' observes Krazy Kow, from her upside-down position. 'Do you think you could stop bouncing quite so hard? You're making all my bits wobble and it's rather uncomfortable.'

'BUT UNITED ARE LOSING!!' screams Bromley, red with effort.

'So I see,' says Krazy Kow, calmly. 'I have noticed in these games that when one side wins, the other side loses.'

Bromley stops in mid bounce and falls back on the sofa. He gives Krazy Kow a Deeply Puzzled look.

Bromley Spottiswood has three facial expressions. He can do Deeply Puzzled (self-explanatory), Raaaargh! (rage), and Wow! I'm Excited! (You guessed it). His most common look is definitely Deeply Puzzled.

(Is he based on my very own Big Bro? Would I do such a thing? Of course not!)

'But of course one side loses when the other side wins,' grunts Bromley.

'Then why go off your head about it?' asks Krazy Kow quietly. 'You know it's going to happen one way or the other.'

'BECAUSE UNITED ARE NOT SUPPOSED TO LOSE!!' roars Bromley, who is now doing Expression Number Two.

The door opens and Big
Sister swirls into the room.
Gosforth has painted her lips
deep purple. Her
false eyelashes
are so huge and
heavy that she
can barely open
her eyes. She slowly
makes her way across the room, arms stretched out
like an Ancient Egyptian mummy as she stumbles
into the furniture and bangs into the sofa..

(Is she based on my big sister? Would I do such
a thing? Of course not!)

'WATCH YOURSELF!' yells Bromley, not taking
his eyes off the flickering screen.

Krazy Kow glances up at Gosforth and her big
pink tongue almost falls out of her mouth with
alarm.

'Goodness, Gosforth, you did give me a shock!'

Gosforth smiles a happy purple smile. 'Yeah! I
look great, don't I?'

[*Phweep! Phweep! Phweep! Phweep!*]

The red light sitting on top of
the telly suddenly begins
to flash and the alarm
sounds. The screen
flickers and a Special
Report comes on.

Calling Krazy Kow!

'Calling Krazy Kow!
Calling Krazy Kow! This is
the International Emergency, Help,
Somebody Do Something Quickly Committee. We
have a Major Nuclear Disaster in Australia!'

'I HATE IT WHEN THAT HAPPENS!!' screams
Bromley. 'NOW I WON'T KNOW IF UNITED LOST.'

'You can always find out later,' Krazy Kow points
out.

'LATER IS TOO LATE,' Bromley bellows,
pummelling the sofa with his fists.

'Well, I'm afraid there is a world disaster going on
and I must go and sort it out,' says Krazy Kow.

'I DON'T CARE ABOUT WORLD DISASTERS!! I
WANT TO KNOW IF UNITED LOST. THAT'S THE
BIGGEST DISASTER EVER.'

'If I don't sort this out then there will be no United, or anything else.' Krazy Kow frowns. 'See what it says? Nuclear reactor on fire in Australia, and it's going to explode.' The superhero leaps to her feet. 'I must go there immediately. This is a job for Krazy Kow! To the bathroom and beyond!'

[Very exciting music – the Krazy Kow theme tune (soon to be a best-selling No.1 hit):
Dooooo-bee doodle-oo, diddle-iddle-eeee, diddly-dum-bee-dum-bee-dum, widdly-tiddly-deee etc.]

Scene Three

Krazy Kow hurries upstairs to the bathroom and locks herself in. She slaps on some underleg deodorant and brushes her teeth. She combs the chunky bit between her ears, does a quick flick with the lipstick, tosses her Krazy Kape behind her shoulders, struggles into her udderpants, pulls on her pink diamanté eye mask to make sure that nobody can recognize her, opens the window and gets stuck halfway through.

[Sound effect: something like a squeaky cork being pulled from a bottle]

'I keep telling them to get this window enlarged, urrrh!'

she pants, at last squeezing through.

   [Pop!]

And with a whizz and a pat and a supersonic bang
she is on her way to the Southern Hemisphere.

**'Like a rocket into the blue!
She's black and white – she's Krazy Moooo!'**

Scene Four

The fire is raging furiously. It seems to come from
every part of the reactor complex and the fire units
can hardly get near it. Helicopters fly overhead
[clatter clatter] spraying water uselessly *[splish
splish splosh]*.

'It's going to explode!' cries the Fire Chief. 'We shall all die!'

'What's that in the sky?' yells the reactor's Director. 'It looks like a meteor.'

'A meteor and a reactor fire,' moans the Fire Chief. 'I want my mummy!'

'It's not a meteor, it's Superman! No, it's

Wonderwoman. No, it's Battleboy, Glittergirl, Marvelmoggy, Dippydog ... oh, I don't know who it ... Wait! It's Krazy Kow – brilliant!' yells the Director. 'Krazy Kow has come to save us.'

[*General fanfare for KK:* **Ta-ra ta-ra ta-ra!**]

A huge cheer goes up from the crowd as Krazy Kow zooms overhead. WHOOOOOSH! She flashes across the sky, trailing sparkling cowpats behind her.

She dives into the nearby sea and sucks up a huge amount of water. Whizzing back to the stricken reactor she takes aim. Her amazing udder spins wildly, clicks into position and a moment later a thunderous cascade of water gushes in every direction. Millions of gallons crash down upon the reactor.

[SSSSSPPLLURRRRRGG!]

The flames sizzle. The flames hiss. The flames die. Another great cheer from the soaking crowd. Some of them fall to their knees.

'The fire is out. The reactor isn't going to explode! Krazy Kow has saved us! Thank you, thank you, Krazy Kow!'

Krazy Kow lands in front of the Director, the Fire Chief and the crowd, as they press forward to thank her.

'It's only my job,' she says modestly, carelessly
tossing her Krazy Kape over one haunch. 'Someone
had to do it, and today it was me. Now I have a
message for you all, so listen carefully. This is what
Krazy Kow says to you: I am the Cow!'

'You are the Cow!' answers the crowd.

Scene Five

Gobb-Yobb Badmash watches the Mappa
Monstrosa in despair. He beats his fists upon his
slimy chest. 'Snirch! Who is this little cweature that
dares to upset my plans for world destwuction?'

'O Dark Contaminator, that is Krazy Kow.'

'A cow? One of those lumpy cweatures that give
milk and cheese and double cweam?'

'Yes, O Great One. She appears to be some kind
of superhero, sent to thwart your evil plans for

turning Earth into Planet Pollution.'

Gobb-Yobb slumps back upon his throne. 'I have been foiled by a daiwy dung dolloper!' He seethes slowly. 'So, we shall see. You may be the Cow, but I am the Pwince of Pestilence, and I shall see you wiped fwom the face of this Earth if it's the last thing I do. Kwazy Kow, your fate is sealed!'

[Camera closes on Gobb-Yobb Badmash looking extremely evil and mightily menacing, slowly slurping on a very long, wriggling worm. More menacing music: **Twannnng! Kwannng! Pwannng! Psssshhh!***]*

It's going to make a brilliant film and I just know that I'm going to be famous. I don't understand how Mr Oldman can't see what a fantastic story it is. I mean surely he didn't really want to know what everyone had done over the weekend? (Answer: They played footie. What a surprise!)

4 The Queen of the Night

The bathroom door opens. Out steps a strange creature, half human, half alien-space-thing from afar, something that has wriggled down a worm hole from the furthest reaches of a parallel universe. It stands in the doorway, blinking in the light, like a startled bat. It is dressed in black from head to toe, cobwebby black. Long black hair hangs down the sides of a moon-pale face. Purple lips pout. Dark eyes stare like tarantulas.

This is my sister, Gemma, dressed like the Queen of the Night. I call her that because she nearly always shrouds herself in black and wanders around the place like a small, loose bit of the night sky that has broken off and somehow come to lodge in our house.

Now, you're probably thinking – Gosforth! Gemma is just like Gosforth! Well, of course she is! That's half the fun of making up all this stuff. You make up things in your head about all the people you know, especially the people you don't like much. Then you make things happen to them. It's great fun.

Having said that, I like Gemma, even though she's a bit odd. I mean, she dresses like someone who wants to dance in graveyards at midnight and drink bat's blood. She thinks it makes her look Interesting and Intense. Mum and Dad are always going on at her. They tell her she looks like a ghoul. Big Bro thinks she looks like a ghoul. I think she looks like a ghoul, but I can't say that because then I'd be agreeing with Mum and Dad and Big Bro. Anyhow, I like ghouls. I'm going to make films with ghouls in them. I could make Gemma a star. I can hear the voice-over:

Here she comes, drifting down the darkened stairway, her

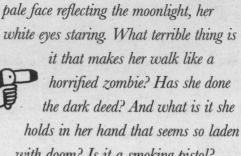

*pale face reflecting the moonlight, her
white eyes staring. What terrible thing is
it that makes her walk like a
horrified zombie? Has she done
the dark deed? And what is it she
holds in her hand that seems so laden
with doom? Is it a smoking pistol?
Aaarghh! Run for it!*

Just a sec, it's OK, it's her
hairdryer. Oh no, not more split
ends.

Amazingly, although Gemma
looks like a ghoul most of the
time, she is also an air cadet
and she goes to Air Cadets twice a week. The
cadets have a special training area next to our
school. One evening she has training, and on the
next she goes to band practice. She plays the
trumpet. She wears a uniform, with a beret and a
badge and she puts highly polished shoes on her
feet and off she goes to train, or to blow her
trumpet.

This is what I find odd about Gemma. The air

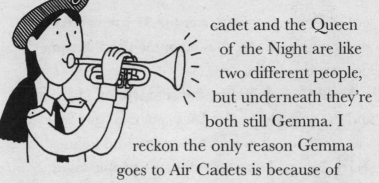

cadet and the Queen
of the Night are like
two different people,
but underneath they're
both still Gemma. I
reckon the only reason Gemma
goes to Air Cadets is because of
Justin. You could say that Justin is her boyfriend,
only she won't admit it. She says: 'We play in the
band together, that's all.'

Justin plays the triangle.
Apparently it's more difficult
than it looks, so Gemma
reckons. She says he's the
best triangle player they
have. I asked her how many
triangle players there were in
the band. She just looked at
me, like I was being awkward, but
I only asked. Honestly, she's so sensitive.

It's funny though, I suppose we've got
something in common, me and Gemma. Nobody
understands me either, but at least Mum and Dad

let Gemma get on with her life. If I start talking about making films, they treat me like I'm some kid with daydreams.

I told Gemma about the competition at school and she asked me what I was going to do for it. I was dying to tell her, but I wanted it to be a secret. I guess I was afraid that if people knew what I was planning they'd just laugh at me.

'You can tell me,' Gemma urged. 'I promise I won't let on.'

So I spilled the beans. Gemma sat on the edge of my bed and listened. She asked a few questions, like what did Gobb-Yobb Badmash look like, and why did Krazy Kow live with an ordinary family?

When I finished she sat back against the wall. Do you know what she said?

'That's a really good idea, Jamie. I think it might even win. You go for it!'

I shrugged.

'Well, I think your school would be mad if they don't use your idea. It's different and funny and exciting. Where do you get your ideas from?'

'They just seem to appear inside my head.'

Gemma smiled. 'Must be pretty weird inside there,' she said, and I knew she meant it as a compliment. After all, this was the girl who dressed like a vampire to impress people.

'You won't tell anyone?' I insisted.

Gemma held up both hands. 'Not a soul.' She gave me a very serious look. 'You've got to enter, Jamie.'

'Mrs Drew is going to tell us which project has been chosen at the end of this week. She was telling us about the judges for the competition. One of them is going to be Kooky Savage.'

'Kooky Savage!' Now Gemma was even more impressed. I was pretty sure she would be. Kooky Savage is a film star and she's Gemma's heroine. Gemma's room is plastered with pictures of her.

'I'd love to be Kooky Savage,' Gemma said dreamily.

'Yeah, I know. I want to be Steven Spielberg.'

Gemma gave a little laugh and patted me. 'You will be, Jamie, you will be. Good luck with your idea.'

As she got off the bed I asked her if we would ever see her boyfriend.

'You don't think I'd ever bring Justin to this house, do you?' she said, her whole mood changing.

'Ah! So he is your boyfriend?'

'I never said he was.'

'You never said he wasn't.'

Gemma stood halfway across the room, looking at me. I could tell she wanted to say something, so I waited.

'OK, you told me about Krazy Kow, so I'll tell you about Justin. Yes, he's my boyfriend, but don't you dare tell Mum or Dad or Matt.'

I grinned at her.

'Have you kissed him, then?'

Gemma's face went scarlet! It was wonderful! She tried to pull herself up tall and haughty. 'THAT is none of your business,' she said, and

swept from the room. (In other words – yes, they had!)

After she'd gone I lay back on my bed and grinned at the ceiling. I'd always liked Gemma, and those things she had said about Krazy Kow – that was really good. I don't know if anyone has ever said anything like that to you, but it makes you feel as if all your insides have just been given a big cuddle. I know it sounds soppy, but that's how it is. It makes you feel pretty good. It's nice to know there's someone who's on your side, someone who understands. After all, nobody else did.

There was no point in telling the rest of the family about Krazy Kow anyway, because they were completely taken up with Big Bro. Matt had got a letter. He'd been called up for a trial for the county football team.

'I'm gonna be in the county team!' he sang at the top of his voice.

'You've done us proud, son,' said Dad.

He was grinning from ear to ear. 'The county team! You could play for United one day! I always said you were brilliant.'

I thought: Yeah. You've always said he was brilliant. And you've always said I was … what? What have you told me, Dad? Not a lot, really.

Do you ever get that feeling you don't belong? Like maybe you were switched at birth in hospital, that you don't belong to your family at all?

'When's the trial?' I asked.

'Two weeks,' shouted Matt. 'Tom Hardy's been called up too.'

'Oh good.'

'You could sound a bit more enthusiastic, Jamie.' This was my mother.

'I'm going in for a competition too,' I said.

'What competition is this?' asked Dad.

'It's some stupid thing about the environment,' Matt explained. 'Mrs Drew wants everyone to have a go.'

'But you've got football practice,' Dad said.

'I know. It's not me who's going in for it. It's Jamie.' Matt turned his sneering face on me. 'You haven't got a hope. You couldn't win an egg and spoon race even if they glued the egg to the spoon for you.'

Dad smiled at me. 'Going to make another film?'

It was the way Dad said 'another film', knowing perfectly well that I hadn't made any film at all yet, that all I did was talk about them. To him it was all talk. Things were so simple for him and Matt. They'd say: 'Let's play football.' And they'd go and play football. But you can't just say: 'Let's make a film,' and then go and do it. So I left the room.

I felt as if someone had just dumped a truckful of anger deep inside me somewhere. Making a film wasn't a joke to me. It was real. This was going to be my big opportunity, and Gemma had helped me to make up my mind.

I'm going to show them all, I thought. I'm going to do it.

5 Krazy Kow and the Exploding Strawberries

Scene One

Breakfast at the Spottiswoods: Krazy Kow lazes in her chair, crossing her back legs and letting out a satisfied sigh.

'Yum yum, strawberries for breakfast.' She dangles a strawberry above her fat pink lips and drops it in. 'Mmmmmmmm!'

> *[Munch munch munch]*

Gosforth glances across at the supercow. 'You

have strawberries every morning. Don't you ever get bored?'

Krazy Kow clasps her front legs behind her head and leans back further. 'Cows eat grass, Gosforth. Have you ever tried eating grass?'

'Of course not. I'm not a cow.'

'You are,' mutters Bromley.

'I heard that, Matchbox-Brain.' Krazy Kow looks at them with disappointment. 'Children, children! Brothers and sisters should love each other dearly.'

(Sorry about this, but it's just the sort of daft thing my mum says to Matt and me when we quarrel.)

Bromley and Gosforth splutter into their cereal bowls. 'Love each other? You must be joking!' they chorus.

Krazy Kow raises one eyebrow. 'As I was saying, cows eat grass. We have it for breakfast, lunch and tea. If we want a snack between meals, we have grass. If we want a midnight feast, we have grass. Quite frankly, it gets rather boring after a while. But strawberries! Oh happy day!'

> [High and happy tinkly music: ***Tinkly winkly winkly wee!*** *that slowly but surely changes into dark and nasty jangly music:* ***Nang-nangy-nang! Twing-twongy-twanng!! Dayayayayayayayayinnnggg!!!***]

Scene Two

As Castle Corruption floats above the bleak wastelands of Antarctica, Gobb-Yobb Badmash stares into the Mappa Monstrosa. A slow smile

spreads like a plague
across his face. It is a
twisted, cruel, sneering,
scar of a smile.

'Stwawbewwies!' he
cries. 'Stwawbewwies
will bwing about the
downfall of that
widiculous cow. I have
an idea, Snirch, and it is
wather good.'

'I'm sure it is, Plague-
Master,' fawns Snirch. 'Do tell.'

'We shall gwow some genetically modified
stwawbewwies, especially for KK. I shall make them
manufacture their own high explosive. Moments
after she swallows them – BANG! Poor Kwazy Kow,
she'll be blown to bits.'

 [*Huge orchestra plays massive dark chords:*
  Ba-ba-ba-baaaaaaa!]

'A breakfast bomb,' cries Secretary Snirch.
'Snap! Crackle! Pop!'

'Quite so. And to make it even better, the force of

the explosion will be so gweat that the entire stweet will be blown to bits with her. Won't Kwazy Kow be surpwised!'

'Won't Krazy Kow be surprised,' echoes Snirch, with a satisfied chuckle.

So Gobb-Yobb works away in his laboratory, producing the perfect Exploding Strawberry. He tests it on Secretary Snirch's teddy. Snirch is not too happy about this, and the teddy is even less pleased, as it is blown up.

Arms and legs and one glass eye shoot across the laboratory.

> [Sound effects: Spinning legs and bouncing eye: *twooooweee-oooweee-oooweee-ooowoeee-oooweee, boing boing boing boing!*]

'Success!' cries Gobb-Yobb, as bits of stuffing drift slowly down through the air, like swollen snow.

'Yes, Master,' sighs Snirch, quietly gathering together the bits and pieces of his scattered teddy.

That night he sits up late in his bedroom, sewing the teddy back together. He is only partly successful.

The exploding strawberries are carefully packed into a box and given a label:

A TASTE SENSATION!
THEY'LL EXPLODE
IN YOUR MOUTH!

Gobb-Yobb hands them over to a Mashman and sends him down with instructions to put them where Krazy Kow is bound to see them.

*[Manic echoing laughter: **hee hee hee hee hee!!**]*

Scene Three

'It's shopping time,' says
Mrs Spottiswood. 'Who's
coming to the supermarket?'

'Not me,' says Gosforth, who is
busy painting her fingernails black.

'Not me,' chorus Bromley and his dad. They are
busy watching a film about how United become
undercover spies during the Second World War,
break the secret code being used by the enemy,
invent the Spitfire, sink the Bismarck and Save the
World from Tyranny.

Krazy Kow watches as the football team
somehow manages to beat off eighty-three enemy
tanks, twelve thousand charging troops, an entire
bomber squadron and win the war.

'United are the best!' sighs Bromley.

'You don't believe all that, do you?' asks Krazy Kow.

'Of course. It's true, you know.'

'It's a film,' says Krazy Kow. 'It's made up.'

'I know it's made up, but it's still true,' insists Bromley.

Krazy Kow goes cross-eyed and shakes her head rapidly in despair, her tongue flopping about like a mad dishcloth. Brrrrrrrrrrrr!

Scene Four

[At the supermarket – background shopping music with voice-over: 'And just for today we have reduced our cabbages. That's right! Instead of being as big as a cabbage should be they are now the same size as apples, but they're still the same price! Isn't that

fantastic? Come and get your reduced
cabbage now.']

By the time Krazy Kow and Mrs Spottiswood
reach the supermarket KK has calmed down. She
has a nice time, wandering around the aisles with her
handbag, trolley and shopping list.

'Underleg deodorant, wrinkle cream, bubble bath …'

Little old ladies keep popping over to ask for her
autograph and see if she's had any good adventures
lately.

'You're my role model,' one of them tells her.
'You are the Cow!'

'You're not supposed to recognize me,' hisses
KK. 'Why do you think I wear a mask over my eyes
when I'm on a mission?'

Krazy Kow doesn't notice that everywhere she goes she is quietly shadowed by a very short, fat man wearing dark tights and a black polo-neck sweater with MASHMAN written across the front. (Most people think it's a designer label.) He also wears a huge cape, with something hidden beneath it.

[*Every time the Mashman appears you hear music like when the shark appears in* Jaws: ***Duh-duh duh-duh duh-duh duh-duh ...***]

'I must get some cream for my udder,' KK tells Mrs Spottiswood. 'I had to use my flame thrower last night and it's rather sore.'

'Try Plum de ma Tante Moisturizer,' suggests Mrs Spottiswood, before going off to get some reduced cabbage because it is on Special Offer and that means it is special.

After that Krazy Kow sets off to find some strawberries. As she approaches the fruit and vegetable selection the Mashman hurries ahead of her. He slips a box of strawberries on to the front of the display, steps back, and waits.

Krazy Kow reads the label on the box and licks her lips. 'Hmmm. Those look very nice. I shall have those for breakfast,' and she slips them into her trolley.

OH NO!

Scene Five

Gobb-Yobb Badmash, the Dark Contaminator, gazes into the Mappa Monstrosa and claps his hands. Soon Krazy Kow will be no more.

[Dark and jangly music again – the Gobb-Yobb theme tune]

Scene Six

Krazy Kow gets home and she is putting the strawberries into the fridge when she realizes that she just cannot resist having one straight away. She chooses the biggest strawberry of all and pops it into her mouth.

'This is lovely,' says Krazy Kow. 'The best strawberry I've had for ages.'

[Munch munch munch]

The strawberry slips down her throat. Shlurppy-shlippp. Just as it reaches Stomach Number One –

The whole of Krazy Kow's body leaves the ground, hits the ceiling and lands again.

'A taste explosion!' cries Krazy Kow, and she burps. A puff of dark smoke drifts across the top of her tongue.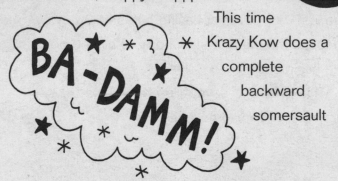

On goes the strawberry to Stomach Number Two. Shlurppy-shlippp …

This time Krazy Kow does a complete backward somersault

and lands flat on the floor.

'Oh yummy yum!' she cries. 'That is the best strawberry ever!'

The strawberry slips into Stomach Number Three. Shlurppy-shlippp…

BA-BA-BANGG!!!

It explodes again, and Krazy Kow finds herself stuck to the ceiling for several seconds, before she comes crashing back down on the table. She gives herself a good shake. Brrrrrrrrrrrrrr! Smoke pours from her ears, and one or two other places.

'Oh heaven!' she sighs. 'That was so nice!'

And then the strawberry reaches Stomach Number Four. Shlurrpy-shlippp…

BA-BA-BOO-BOOM!!!

Krazy Kow shoots around the room five times, like a giant escaped balloon. Flames come roaring from her rear end as she is jet-propelled around the kitchen, with her tail spinning at several thousand miles an hour.

> [Sound effect: jet engine mixed with kitchen equipment crashing and smashing]

Suddenly a miniature parachute-brake pops out and slows her down. She crash-lands in a chair, where she sits with a delighted smile on her face.

'That was some strawberry,' she tells Gosforth, who has just put her head into the kitchen to see what all the noise is about. 'And something tells me that strawberries don't normally have that effect. I think someone has just tried to blow me up.'

Krazy Kow goes to the fridge. She carefully sniffs the strawberries and examines them with the molecular microscope hidden in her horns.

'Aha. I thought as much. These have been genetically modified to explode,' she says. 'If you had eaten these, Gosforth, they would have killed you, and lots of other people too. It's a good thing I have a superhero's stomach – standard issue, you know. I had better dispose of these safely.'

Scene Seven

Krazy Kow grabs the strawberries. 'To the bathroom and beyond!' she cries and with a whizz and a pat and a supersonic bang she zooms into the safety of the sky.

'Like a rocket into the blue!
She's black and white –
she's Krazy Moooo!'

Krazy Kow hurls the box of strawberries as far as she can into the upper atmosphere. She turns on her back, lifts one rear leg, expertly spins her udder, clicks it into position and *[FFWWHISSHHH!]*

a miniature missile shoots out and hits the strawberries, dead on.

[KAPPOWWW!!! SPPINNGG!!! SHADDANNGGG!!!
FWIZZZZ!!!!! BADOOMM!!!!!]

Strawberries rocket up into the sky and explode, raining juice down on passing cars and people. More strawberries plaster the walls of the surrounding houses, but at least everyone is safe.

['Strawberries-are-raining-on-my-head'-type music]

An excited, strawberry-bespattered crowd gathers outside the Spottiswood house. 'You have saved us from the Exploding Strawberries, Krazy Kow. Thank you, thank you!'

Krazy Kow quickly adjusts her lipstick and holds up her front legs for silence.

'It was nothing,' she cries. 'I am here to help you at all times. Now listen to me, I have a message for you. This is what I say: I am the Big Moo!'

'You are the Big Moo!' cheers the crowd. 'Hurrah!'

Scene Eight

High in Castle Corruption, Gobb-Yobb Badmash fumes. 'I shall get you, Kwazy Kow. I SHALL get you!'

He plunges his hands into his pockets and pulls out two large wriggling clumps of worms. He stuffs them into his mouth.

[Boo-hiss-what's-he-going-to-do-next? kind of music]

6 I Get the Job

I worked really hard on Krazy Kow. I borrowed
Mum's computer and got it all written up tidily. I
put the pages and all my drawings into a neat
plastic folder and handed them in to Mrs Drew.
After that all I could do was wait.

Mrs Drew made the announcement in
Assembly a few days later. She thanked everybody
for their hard work. 'But I can only choose one
project to submit,' she said, and I was thinking:
We know that – get on with it! My heart was
pounding. 'All the staff have taken a look at your
ideas and I have to say that there was one idea
that really stood out. The winner is Jamie Frink,
from Class J5.'

It was me! I always knew it would happen. I
was on my way to fame and fortune. I was already
famous in my school. It was as if everyone was

looking at me. I could see Matt's face – totally stupefied. Somewhere in the background Mrs Drew was still talking, telling them about Krazy Kow and how she fights Gobb-Yobb Badmash. I was grinning from ear to ear. I couldn't stop myself. When Assembly was finished I walked back to class in a kind of dream. Most of my classmates were already there, looking puzzled. I grinned at them.

'A cow?' said Rebecca, tossing back her long, blonde hair like a slow-mo shampoo ad. (You too can have hair like Rebecca – washed in a mountain stream; using pongy weed and toad bits. You can live the dream!) 'Why a cow?'

'That's how it came to me,' I explained.

'It's silly,' she announced, and my heart sank. Beautiful Rebecca thought it was silly. I tried to explain that Krazy Kow was meant to be silly. I suppose I should have kept quiet at this point, but I couldn't resist going on. Getting Mrs Drew's support had made me feel really good about the whole thing.

'Listen, I'm going to be a famous film director one day. This is just the start.'

Rebecca looked at me as if I'd gone totally off my head and began a slow, hollow laugh. Then she delivered her final verdict.

'That is so pretentious!'

Everyone started sneering and laughing at me, even though none of us knew what it meant! I don't suppose even Rebecca knew what it meant. She was always coming out with long words. It didn't mean she understood them. It was the way she said them. And she said 'pretentious' as if it meant dog poo, or quite probably something bigger than that, like elephant poo. Maybe even brontosaurus poo.

Then the others waded in with their little bits of criticism.

'Yeah, and who wants to save the world anyway?' interrupted Carl.

'So what would you rather do?' I asked. 'Play football?'

Silence. They didn't want to answer that one. A single voice spoke up.

'Save the world, of course.' We all turned to see who it was. Cat blushed very red and scowled back. ('Cat' was short for Catherine, and also because she had green, slanted eyes. Her small nose and short spiky hair only added to the impression.) 'Jamie's right,' she insisted. 'Pollution is a big problem. The idea of Krazy Kow is a really good way to get the message across.'

'Oh look,' sneered Rebecca, 'it's the film director's assistant.'

A sniggering chorus went up from the boys.

'Oooooh!' One of them made kissy noises and they laughed. At last they moved off, leaving me alone with Cat, who was now crimson. She gazed up at me. (Cat's actually pretty short, the shortest in our class. She has to gaze up at everyone.)

'They're just jealous,' she said. 'I like your idea. It's different. All I did was write about polluting the planet, but a film – that's brilliant.'

'Thank you.'

'You're really clever.'

'Not really.'

'Oh come on, you are. Nobody else thought of a cartoon cow.'

I smiled. It was nice of Cat to say all this, but I was beginning to feel embarrassed.

'I can help you with it.'

'Yeah?' I wasn't too sure about this. My street cred was already pretty low. In the distance I could see Rebecca, watching. She was laughing at us.

'We could work on it together.'

'Er, I don't need much help at the moment, thanks.'

'I don't mind. I could just hang around,' suggested Cat. 'In case you need anything.' She looked at me and her eyes reminded me of an eager puppy. I didn't want an eager puppy.

'I don't think I will be needing anything.'

The smile quickly faded and Cat chewed at her lower lip. I thought she was going to say more, but she just shoved her hands into her pockets, shrugged and walked off. Strange girl. I almost called out to her. I wanted to know if she knew what pretentious meant.

Soon after this I was called in to see Mrs Drew. She had some good news and some bad news.

'Jamie, you mustn't let anyone else know yet, but the organizers have been so impressed by some of the ideas sent in by schools that some of the judges are going to make special visits to see the work being done.'

'You mean they might come to our school?'

Mrs Drew nodded and leaned forward, almost whispering, 'They *are* going to come to our school. I've been told to expect two of them in a week's time.'

My eyes were boggling. 'Which ones?' I asked.

'Kooky Savage and Dwight Trellis.'

'The film star …?' I began.

'… and the United winger. Isn't that fantastic?'

I couldn't believe it. The thought of having Kooky Savage in my own school – a real film star. Somebody who worked in real films with real directors. Somebody who might one day STAR IN A FILM BEING MADE BY ME!

Just as I was getting nicely carried away with my little dream, Mrs Drew brought me back to Earth with a bang. It turned out that she wanted to make a film of Krazy Kow all right, but not a cartoon.

'We don't have the facilities, Jamie. You need special cameras for that.'

'Can't we get them?'

'I'm sorry. We don't have the time or the

money. But I do think we can make a really good film about Krazy Kow. I've got hold of a cow costume.'

What?! My brilliant cartoon character was being turned into a pantomime cow!

'It's the best we can do. Wait until you see it. I've set up the video camera in the hall and gathered some of the children together so that we can try it out.'

I sighed heavily. 'Can I at least do the filming?'

'I don't see why not. I thought your brother and Tom Hardy could be the front and back of the cow.'

I didn't know whether to laugh or cry. The thought of two ace footballers inside a cow costume just seemed so weird – and it would serve them right!

We went off to the hall and there in a corner lay three large, black and white crumpled heaps – the front, back and head bits of a cow. The rest of the cast were gathered round them.

'We're going to film the first episode,' began Mrs Drew. 'This is where Krazy Kow discovers a nuclear reactor on fire. Matt and Tom, you get in the cow. Carl, help them hook together, will you? Tom, your udder's not on straight. Pull it up between your knees. That's better. Matt, can you stop twisting round?'

'Tom poked me,' said Matt, his voice muffled by the big cow head he was wearing.

'Didn't.'

'Did.' The front half of the cow swung round and aimed a kick at the back half.

'Ow!' The back section launched itself at the front, wrestling it to the ground, where the two halves rolled about thumping each other. The sound of laughter came from inside. Mrs Drew puffed over to the wriggling cow. 'Boys, please!' Krazy Kow's tail twitched and Tom poked his head out of a gap in the middle where the costume joined up. 'Sorry,' he muttered, trying to appear serious. I knew he was deliberately playing up. He was trying to sabotage my film.

'That's all right, Tom. Pick yourselves up, both of you, and get yourselves sorted.' Mrs Drew heaved another sigh. 'Now, is everyone set?'

'Camera's running,' I called out, and focused on Krazy Kow. Her head suddenly twisted round.

'Will you stop poking? Ow!' Now the front half of Krazy Kow suddenly leaped in the air and yanked off her own head. Matt was trying to look cross, but there was a big grin hidden beneath his frown.

'Now what?' demanded Mrs Drew.

'Tom pinched my bum!'

'Don't be daft, I've got a bum of my own.'

Everyone in the hall fell about. 'Anyhow,' Tom went on, 'you could have pinched your own ...'

'Sssssh! Please! Do be quiet!' cried Mrs Drew. 'Tom, Matthew, will you behave? We have filming to do. Jamie, are you ready?'

'I've been ready for years.'

'There's no need for sarcasm, thank you.' Mrs Drew took a deep breath. 'OK, everyone, ready, action!'

Krazy Kow began to clump across the hall. 'A nuclear fire in Australia!' bellowed Matt from inside the cow's head. 'Oh no! I must fly into action. Argh! Stop it! Ow!'

The front half of

Krazy Kow began jumping up and down and then all of a sudden took off across the hall. The back half couldn't keep up, tripped and fell to the floor, only to be dragged along behind the front as it raced away.

Tom was spun on to his back and his front and his back again, until his legs and tail and great pink udder were waving about like some gigantic rubber glove. Round and round went Matt, while Tom polished the hall floor, swishing about in great swinging arcs, until at last the cow ripped in half. The back end went spinning across the hall floor and crashed into the wall. Tom poked out his head.

'Have you quite finished?'

'You started it,' snapped Matt.

'That's enough!' cried Mrs Drew. 'Both of you go back to your classroom.' She watched, hands on hips, as the two boys slunk away, smirking at each other.

Mrs Drew put another two children in the cow and we started again. After that the filming went smoothly, but – and it was a very big BUT – it wasn't what I wanted. It wasn't anything like what I had imagined in my head. It wasn't even anything like the stories I had written down. A pantomime cow simply was not Krazy Kow. My dreams were crumbling to bits all around me.

After school I was heading for home when Cat caught up with me. She fell in alongside, panting from running.

'Wasn't much good, was it?'

I grunted.

'They're useless, that lot. They haven't got any imagination. They can't see what you and I can see.'

I grunted again. So, Cat thought she knew what was going on inside my head, did she? I had this sudden mad picture in my head of Krazy Kow leaping through the air, her Swiss army udder firing off in every direction. I mean, nobody's head is like that, except mine!

'Why don't you make your own film?' Cat suggested. 'Forget about the school film. Make your own cartoon, the way you want it to be.'

I kept on walking. This was a surprisingly good

suggestion from Cat.

'Well?' She was half running beside me, bouncing up and down, trying to keep up.

'It's not that easy.'

'I could help you. We could do it together.'

This was the second time Cat had offered to help. She was watching me earnestly, but that puppy-dog look had gone. She meant business. I stopped.

'OK. You can help, but I'm in charge and you do what I say.'

Cat's face cracked into a massive smile. 'Brilliant!' She suddenly flung both arms round me and gave me a huge hug. 'Gerroff!' I yelled.

7 Too Many Strawberries

Dad's got a video camera he uses for filming Big Bro when he's playing football. Dad reckons it's good for training. They sit and watch it for hours, replaying special moves. I reckoned I could make my film with Dad's camera. I don't think he's used it for weeks and although he's the only one allowed to handle it I was sure I could get away with it, so I grabbed the thing.

Once I was up in my bedroom I examined the camera because I wanted to make sure I knew how it worked. I pointed it out of the window and peered through, finger on the button. And that was when I saw Gemma, with Justin.

They were kissing!

There they were, in the little alley that runs along the back of our garden, where they thought nobody would spot them. I could only see their

heads, but it was definitely Gemma and Justin. It was as if their lips had been superglued together. I kept the button pressed. It just seemed the thing to do. It was like I was a great news photographer, right on the spot, just as the big news was breaking.

HEADLINE FLASH – GEMMA SNOGS JUSTIN!

After they'd gone I played the tape back.

Something about it didn't seem right, and then I realized what it was: there was no soundtrack. So I switched on the microphone and sat there making loads of really shlurpy shloppy kissy-kissy noises. It sounded disgusting and I must admit it gave me a bit of a laugh, but I had more important things to think about.

I wanted to start filming the Krazy Kow story, starting with the exploding strawberries. The question that was bothering me was – how do you make strawberries explode? And how do you film it at the same time? I spent the entire weekend thinking about it. I thought my brain would burst, it was so full of cows and strawberries and cameras. But by the time I went to bed on Sunday night I reckoned I had worked out what to do.

I spoke to Cat about it the next day and told her we were going to film the episode with the exploding strawberries.

'Where are you going to get exploding strawberries from?'

'The exploding strawberry shop,' I said.

'No, really, how will you do it?' She laughed and pushed me.

I smiled and tapped my nose. Cat scowled furiously.

'Tell me!'

'Come to my house after school tomorrow. Matt will be out training and Gemma goes to Air

Cadets so there won't be anyone else around for a while. We can get the filming done then.'

'But I still don't see how …'

'Just come tomorrow.'

I hurried off. I had so much to sort out. This filming business was taking over my life. I already had a stupendous idea for the exploding strawberries, but there were other things I needed too, like Krazy Kow herself.

Down in the toddlers' classrooms they have loads of stuffed toys, and I had a vague memory that one of them was a black and white cow. So I snuck down there, only to run straight into one of the dinner ladies, Mrs Bevinson.

It's pretty easy to run into Mrs Bevinson because she's about three miles wide and made of old mattresses. Well, that's what she looks like, at any rate. Mrs Bevinson always walks very slowly, like a robot with a battery that's running down, her tiny, rolling-pin arms swinging at her sides. She's so wide she fills the school corridors like some minesweeper. I couldn't help but run straight into her.

'Oi! I know you!' she thundered, as I struggled
to free myself from her Venus flytrap bosom.
'What do you think you're up to?'

My brain was on holiday somewhere. What I
really needed at this moment was for Krazy Kow
herself to appear in the corridor and zap Mrs
Bevinson with her flame-thrower. Barbecued
dinner lady. Stay calm, I told myself. Do not
flinch at the Jaws of Death. Be Hercules. Be
Indiana Jones. Be Mr Cool.

I smiled at Mrs Bevinson. 'I lost my jacket

yesterday. One of the teachers said she thought she saw it hanging on a peg in the cloakroom down here.'

Mrs Bevinson took a step back and squinted at me with one eye. 'YOU'RE JUST TRYING IT ON!' she bellowed. (This is Mrs Bevinson's favourite phrase. Whatever anyone says to her she answers: 'You're just trying it on!')

I stayed quiet and kept my eyes on hers. She grunted and moved to one side, as far as she was able. I tunnelled past her and disappeared into the cloakroom while she carried on out to the playground, heaving like an overloaded car ferry.

As soon as she was out of sight I slipped into the toddlers' classroom and dived in among the soft toys. It took only a few moments to find the little cow. I stuffed it in my bag and hurried off. (I was going to take it back later. That was my plan.)

When Cat arrived at the house she was beaming with excitement. 'Is this where you live?' she asked. Since I'd just answered the front door this struck me as a pretty weird question.

'We're going to film in the kitchen,' I told her, and she followed me through to the back of the house. I had already cleared the kitchen table and set up the video camera on a tripod at one end.

'Ignore the washing hanging up. It's Big Bro's football kit,' I told Cat, and added bitterly: 'Must have him looking his best for the county trial.'

Cat wrinkled her nose at the washing. 'You're not into football much, are you?'

'Nope.'

She smiled. 'Nor me. I hate it. What else do you hate? I hate that too.' She stopped suddenly. 'Sorry, I'm rabbiting. What are we going to do?'

I'd got hold of all the strawberries from the fridge and piled them on a paper plate. Underneath the plate was my hydro-helicopter. Connected to the hydro-copter was one of those air pumps operated by foot.

You pump really hard and a huge amount of pressure is stored up in the launch pad. When the pressure gets too much it is suddenly released – PHWOOOSH! – and the helicopter goes zooming up in the air with its rotors whizzing at a million miles an hour.

I stuck Krazy Kow on the table and bent her legs so that it looked as if she might be firing a rocket at the strawberries. 'I'm going to film. You pump as hard as you can. When it takes off the hydro-copter should scatter the strawberries, like they've just exploded. I've got to keep the camera focused on them, without showing the 'copter underneath.'

'Fantastic!' said Cat, clinging on to my arm. 'You're so clever!'

I pulled my arm from her grasp. 'Just do the pumping,' I muttered, and stepped behind the camera. I pressed Record and began a voice-over for Krazy Kow.

'Oh no, these strawberries have been genetically modified to explode. I must dispose of them at once. I shall just use my…'

BAMMMM!!!

The launcher was triggered and the 'copter burst upwards. Strawberries went everywhere. One hit the camera lens head on. Some splattered against the kitchen walls. Some were sliced to bits by the whirling rotor blades. They pummelled into Matt's football kit, leaving massive red blotches on his shorts and socks and shirt. But most of the strawberries hit the ceiling, where they stuck, like squashed supernovas.

The hydro-copter was ricocheting around the kitchen, completely out of control, bouncing off the walls, knocking plants on to the floor and

occasionally trying to decapitate us. At last it plunged into the sink, where it turned the washing-up water into an instant froth of shredded dishcloth and minced geraniums.

The strawberries on the ceiling slowly unstuck themselves and rained down on us, the table, the floor, the washing – each one making a gentle 'splop' as it landed.

I glanced across at Cat. She appeared to be in deep shock, rocking on her feet and dripping strawberry juice. She looked as if she'd just been pulled straight out of a jam pot. All I could see were the whites of her eyes, staring at me.

I grabbed a couple of tea towels and threw one across to Cat. 'Quick, clean up! Mum's going to kill me.'

She still didn't move, but I didn't have time to see what was up. The entire kitchen needed my emergency attention.

I cleaned and wiped and mopped until I thought my arms would fall off. I shoved Matt's football kit into the washing machine and stuffed in all the dirty tea towels. By this time Cat was beginning to stir, so while that lot was washing we tidied up the rest of the place as best we could. I discovered most of Krazy Kow spreadeagled against the kitchen window. She'd been blown apart by the explosion. Her head was under the fridge. One leg was on the stove. Her udder was draped over a potted plant like some exotic bloom. I gathered up the bits and put them in a bag.

There wasn't much we could do about the ceiling. I just had to hope that nobody would notice.

Cat stumbled home. I don't know how she was going to explain herself to her parents. Something like: 'Mum, I was just walking along minding my own business and this big dollop of strawberry jam fell out of the sky and landed on top of me.'

Hmmm, maybe.

I put the camera back, scuttled upstairs and hoped that everything would be all right. I passed the time by trying to stitch Krazy Kow back together.

And everything was all right, for a while. When the others came in they were over the moon because someone important from the county team had been there to watch the training, and Matt had been brilliant, and Mr Important must have seen how good Matt was and he was going to be a football ace of the future and a real star!

I thought: No! I'm going to be the star in this family. You wait and see. Krazy Kow is going to be much bigger than any footballer. Krazy Kow is going to take over the world. I just had to stitch her together first.

Dad was rummaging among the shelves. 'You

remember that match against Hillside Junior,
when you almost scored, but hit the crossbar?
Take a look at it again, Matt, on the video and tell
me what you'd do differently this time.'

AAARGH! PANIC STATIONS!

My heart stopped dead. My mouth wouldn't
work. My voice had dried up. That video was full
of exploding strawberries!

'You don't want to watch it now,' I blurted out.
'You've just been watching football.'

'Fresh in the mind,' said Dad. 'It's the last bit I
filmed, so it should be here.'

The TV flickered into life. There was Matt,
running across a field, chasing a ball. For a brief
moment I thought: It's going to be all right.
Maybe the strawberries come much later than
this. Then the film went crackly, the screen
cleared and the next thing everyone saw was:

Gemma.

And Justin.

Snogging.

With the sound effects I'd made.

[Shlurrppy-shlopp kisskisskisskisskissy shlippy shlurrp!]

We stared and stared and stared. It seemed to go on for ever. Mum and Dad and Matt all leaned forward in their chairs, as if to get an even closer view.

'Listen to it,' murmured Mum in a shocked whisper. 'I think they're eating each other.' She turned to Dad. 'Did you know this was going on?'

Dad shook his head.

At that moment the front door opened and Gemma walked in, fresh from her Air Cadet training. 'Hi, everyone! You'll never guess what …' Her voice suddenly broke off as she saw the TV.

'Good evening,' Mum said stiffly.

On telly the two air cadets came up for air. Then they started again. Gemma stared at the TV as if it was the most horrifyingly scary thing she had ever seen. (It was!)

Dad switched off. He got up and gazed steadily at Gemma.

'You've got some explaining to do,' he growled.

Gemma burst into tears and fled the room. Mum went after her, and that left Dad wondering how Gemma had actually come to be filmed, on his camera. He looked at Matt, but Matt had been out playing football. He looked at me. His eyes stayed looking at me. This could prove to be difficult.

8 Gobb-Yobb Sets a Trap

Scene One

Gobb-Yobb Badmash is in a foul mood. He would be stamping up and down Castle Corruption if he had legs, but he's a slug, so he doesn't. No wonder he's in a foul mood. He fixes Secretary Snirch with a malevolent eye.

'Kwazy Kow must die!' he hisses.

'Good idea,' agrees Snirch.

'We must lure her into a twap and eliminate her.'

'Good idea,' nods Snirch.

'We need something to bait the twap.'

'What about someone?' grins Snirch. 'There are two children living with Krazy Kow. Bromley, the boy, is a football fanatic,' he announces, and Gobb-Yobb Badmash claps his little hands with delight.

'A football fan! Oh good, they're always the easiest. We shall send a Mashman to have a little talk with Sidcup ...'

'Bromley,' Snirch corrects the leader.

'... and see how helpful he can be.' Gobb-Yobb sighs and leans back upon his throne. 'I am looking forward to this. Kwazy Kow, your Moment of Doom is coming fast.'

Scene Two

Bromley Spottiswood is standing in front of his bedroom mirror, dressed in full United kit. He twists this way and that, admiring himself. He makes a few pretend kicks, imagining the roar of the delighted crowd as he scores one goal after another.

'You'd make a bwilliant United player,' says a quiet voice. Bromley spins round. There, sitting on his bed, is a Mashman. (In fact it is Gobb-Yobb himself.)

[*The Gobb-Yobb theme tune*]

'Where did you come from? How did you get into my room?'

Gobb-Yobb smiles. 'I came down the chimney, like Father Chwistmas.'

'There isn't a fireplace in my room,' Bromley points out.

'Oh, give us a bweak!' snaps Gobb-Yobb. 'You childwen are so picky these days. It doesn't matter how I got here. This is your lucky day. There is something I can do for you.'

'Oh yes?'

'I can make your dweams come twue.'

'You don't know what my dreams are,' says Bromley.

'You want to be a football star. You want to play for United in the Cup Final and score the winning goal.'

Bromley stares at Gobb-Yobb as if the slug has just read his mind, which of course he has. Gobb-

Yobb is very good at reading minds, especially when they are so small.

'That would be wonderful,' sighs Bromley. 'Can you really do that?'

'Of course. It's not difficult. But in weturn I need a favour fwom you.' Gobb-Yobb leans forward. 'You have a fwend living here with you, a cow.'

'That's right, Krazy Kow.'

'I want to know what her weak spot is.'

'I can't tell you that!'

'Oh dear. I'm so sowwy. Then I can't make you into a football star.'

Hmm, thinks Bromley. This is difficult. He battles with his conscience, and loses, very quickly.

'In that case I will tell you,' says Bromley cheerfully.

'The boy's a pushover,' murmurs Gobb-Yobb to himself. 'He has as much backbone as a jellyfish.'

'Did you say something?'

'Yes, but you won't understand. Ignowance, as people say, is bliss. And before you intewwupt, don't wowwy, you won't understand that either. Now, what is Kwazy Kow's weak spot? Do tell.'

'She is allergic to nuclear chickens.'

'Nuclear chickens?! But there are no such cweatures in the universe!'

'That's why KK is so successful. If there were nuclear chickens, she would be in dead trouble, and by that I mean that she would be in trouble, and dead.'

'Ha ha! The boy has a sense of humour. Well, it's all vewy stwange and intewesting,' mutters Gobb-Yobb. 'I must get to work at once.'

'Hey! What about making me into a football star?'

'Dweam on!' cries Gobb-Yobb. 'I'm an evil villain. Surely you don't expect me to keep my pwomises?'

He vanishes in a puff of smoke.

Bromley sits on his bed. He wonders what Gobb-Yobb will do. Has he betrayed Krazy Kow by telling of her secret weakness? Bromley shakes his head. No. After all, there are no such things as nuclear chickens. They don't exist. Gobb-Yobb Badmash admitted that himself. Bromley smiles. He isn't a traitor at all.

Scene Three

Back at Castle Corruption Gobb-Yobb is over the moon. He has been working on a new invention and now he is presenting it to Snirch for the first time. A strange creature struts before them, pecking at the ground.

[Chicken music and sound effect of pecking]

It looks like a large chicken, except that its body is more in the shape of a cube than anything truly animal. Gobb-Yobb smiles.

'This is the cweature that is going to destwoy

Kwazy Kow once and for all,' he cries. 'I have cweated an atomic cockewel. Behold – Nuclear Weactor Chicken!'

> [*Chicken suddenly lifts head, looks straight at camera, winks and crows.*]

Cock-a-doodle-DOOMMM!!!

Secretary Snirch admires the fabulously foul fowl, while the Dark Contaminator explains the next stage of his dastardly plan.

'We set a twap – let's say a nice enviwonmental accident ...'

'A giant oil tanker leaking millions of gallons of oil into the ocean!' suggests Snirch.

'Possibly. Or maybe an explosion at a chemical factowy that sends poisonous fumes dwifting across the countwyside killing evewything in its path ...'

'Oh yes,' croons Snirch. 'Or we could kill off every single whale and tiger left on the planet ...'

'And the pandas,' adds Gobb-Yobb. 'Don't forget the giant pandas. I hate them: stupid, fat, fluffy things with as much bwain power as a lollipop. I can't understand why humans like them so much. They go nuts over them.' Gobb-Yobb's voice changes to a dreamy sing-song. ' "Ooooh, I want to give it an ickle cuddle. Come and give me a lovely big huggy-wuggy." Blurgh!'

The two evil villains gaze at each other and sigh with pleasure at their sheer nastiness. They are having such fun. Gobb-Yobb smiles dreamily.

'Now, which idea will it be?'

9 Gloria Gives a Helping Hand

Gemma isn't speaking to me any more. She thinks I betrayed her by filming her with Justin, but how was I to know Dad and Mum would see it? It isn't as if I filmed it especially. It was Gemma's fault for getting in the way when I pressed the record button. I tried to say sorry but she spends all her time shut in her room and won't listen. Anyhow, it was a golden opportunity, definitely not to be missed.

I told Cat what had happened and she just thought it was funny, but then Gemma's not her big sister, is she?

I guess I should be glad that Dad never got round to seeing the rest of the film – the bit with the exploding strawberries. He was so cross he chucked away the whole cartridge, so it's bye-bye to my Oscar-winning exploding strawberries, not to mention my brilliant bit of true life drama —

AIR CADETS
IN MID-AIR COLLISION!
STARRING
GEMMA AND JUSTIN

*Don't miss the new romantic horror film from
Jamie Frink: the world's greatest film director.*

Their eyes met, their noses met, their lips met
– and the audience threw up.

See? I just can't help myself. Even though I
know I've really upset Gemma I also know it
makes a brilliant bit of film. I feel pretty bad
about the whole business. I wish I knew how to
make things right with Gemma.

As for Mum, she's terribly worried
about the kitchen. She thinks some
kind of strange mould is creeping
across the ceiling.

'I've never seen anything like it,' she
told our neighbour. 'It's pinky-red,

and it looks like enormous chicken-pox blisters. I think I ought to call in a mould expert.'

'Sounds more like you need a doctor,' murmured the neighbour.

Anyhow, Cat and I are going to have to start all over again.

To make matters worse things are bad at school too. They started off all right. Mrs Drew called me into her office. I stood there wondering what I'd done wrong, but it turned out to be nothing like that.

'I have to tell you, Jamie, Dwight Trellis and Kooky Savage are coming tomorrow. It's so exciting!'

So that bit of news was OK, but it was later that things began to go wrong. We tried to do some more filming, out in the playground. Mrs Drew wanted to have another go at Krazy Kow saving the nuclear reactor. (Exactly! We still haven't managed to film the first episode yet, and the competition entries have to be in by the end of this week, not to mention Dwight Trellis and Kooky Savage coming to watch the whole thing.

Time is running out!)

Anyhow, I had a good idea. I'd been really worried about how badly the filming was going, not to mention the fact that Mrs Drew isn't making Krazy Kow as a cartoon, which is what it's meant to be, so I've sent a copy of my film script to a film company in America, Awesome Productions. They made that fantastic blockbuster Starship Conqueror, with all the amazing special effects. (Remember the collapsing battle-cruiser, the wall of fire, and the multi-headed space-spiders with telescopic legs? Wow!)

They are going to love my idea for Krazy Kow! I'm expecting to hear from them any day now. In fact I wouldn't be surprised if one of their agents was on his way over here right now. He'll draw up outside my house in a super-stretch limo, one of those things with about twenty windows and ten doors down each side. He'll step out in a really sharp suit and when he sees me he'll say: 'Hey!

You must be the one and only Jamie Frink, creator of Krazy Kow. We want to make your film. It's going to be mega. I've a contract here for a million billion trillion dollars.'

And I'll say: 'Hmmm, maybe. I'll think about it.'

No! Not really! I'll say: 'Yippee!' Or even like this: 'YIPPEE!!!'

In the meantime we have been trying to do some more filming at school. We were well organized, so Mrs Drew left us to it. Cat seems to think she is now my Personal Assistant. She's made a clapperboard from a slice of thick card and a ruler. She keeps getting in the way of the camera and shouting, 'Action!'

We were filming a bit where Krazy Kow is attacked by the Mashmen. Half of my class were wearing tights and black polo-neck sweaters, with black bin liners for capes. Meanwhile Krazy Kow was stomping about the playground bellowing, 'I am the Cow! Moo!' at the top of her lungs.

And then, just when it was beginning to look quite exciting, Miss Ghosh brought out her class of four- and five-year-olds in their leotards and pants and tiny vests. (Those little ones look so funny when they're doing PE! They're like miniature wind-up toys that have gone out of control.)

Of course, the first thing the teeny-toddlers see is a large cow being chased by nasty men in black tights and rustling black bin bags flapping behind them. Half of them burst into tears on the spot.

'There are horrible men chasing that poor cow!' cried one little boy, and he promptly sat down in a heap of tears. Half a dozen wind-up toys immediately tripped over him and set up more wailing. This was rapidly turning into a Who-Can-Wail-The-Loudest Competition.

'Come on, let's save that cow!' This came from Gloria, the biggest girl in Miss Ghosh's class. I mean, she was BIG! She was only four years old but she looked more like forty. She had arms with muscles like rolling pins. (I found out later she was Mrs Bevinson's granddaughter.) So Gloria set off after the Mashmen, yelling her battle cry, with fifteen other tiny tots screaming behind her, while the rest of the class sat in the playground going 'boo-hoo' in very loud voices.

The Mashmen stopped and turned to see what was going on. Some of them were laughing. They thought the teeny tots were funny.

'Aren't they sweet?' I heard one say, before he was mown down by fifteen pairs of toddling trainers bent on revenge.

'Children! Children!' cried poor Miss Ghosh,

trying to run after them in six different directions at once. But her class weren't children any longer. They had turned into monstrous trolls, bent on rescuing a poor cow. When the ones sitting down saw how successful the attackers were they hurried to join in. Soon the Mashmen were running for their lives, while Cat raced after them, banging her clapperboard and shouting, 'Cut! Cut!'

A crowd of delighted toddlers mobbed Krazy Kow and patted her sides.

'You're a lovely cow!' they said. 'You can come to our class and have tea.'

At this suggestion Krazy Kow appeared to fold herself in half as the two boys inside clung to each other for safety.

'We don't want any tea,' trembled Carl, up at the front end. Gloria folded her arms across her chest.

'Yes you do,' she insisted. 'Come on.'

(Gloria is one of those Very Helpful Girls. Do you know the kind I mean? She's the sort of person you find next to you when you're having second thoughts about doing something dangerous, like jumping off the top diving board at the swimming pool. 'You can do it, go on. It's easy. You can do it. Just stand nearer the edge. I'll help you. There.' Push. Scream. Splash. Gloria looks down at the body floating in the water. 'Go on then, swim. Can't you hear? Got water in your ears? I said SWIM! No! I didn't say SINK TO THE BOTTOM OF THE POOL! What's the point in drowning, you daft wotsit? You're dead now. You're useless, you are.')

So Gloria was being Very Helpful Indeed, and the two children inside Krazy Kow were scared. 'I really need a wee,' Carl whispered to the back half, but Gloria heard him, and since she was still Being Helpful she promptly grabbed Krazy Kow by one horn.

'Follow me,' she said, dragging the poor cow towards the infant toilets, with Carl almost being

strangled and making dreadful
urrrghaaarrrgh choking
noises. Gloria then
tried to reverse the
protesting moo-cow
through the door of
the girls' toilet. If it hadn't been for Miss Ghosh,
goodness knows what would have happened next.

'Get that cow out of there at once!'

'The cow said she wanted a wee,' Gloria
explained, ramming her knee into Krazy Kow's
chest and giving her a helpful shove backwards.
The wind was knocked from Carl and he
collapsed on the floor, wheezing.

'This is a pretend cow, Gloria. Real cows can't
talk.'

Gloria turned and stared at Krazy Kow, who
slowly began to fall apart in front of her very eyes.
The back half split from the front and Martin
Coggles stumbled out, clutching his nose.

'I've godda dose bleed,' he mumbled, with
blood dripping through his fingers and on to the
floor.

And then Krazy Kow pulled off her head and a cross-eyed Carl managed to blurt out rather huskily: 'I am the Cow!'

Gloria screamed at the bleeding, headless heifer and ran for her life, while Carl gazed up at Miss Ghosh as if he was about to expire on the spot.

'I really do need a …'

'Yes, all right, go!' cried Miss Ghosh. 'The rest of you follow me. PE has been cancelled!'

All around the playground the bruised and trampled Mashmen struggled to their feet. I reckon the world didn't need Krazy Kow any more. Those Mashmen didn't stand a chance. Miss Ghosh's toddlers could save the world, no problem at all.

Mrs Drew came hurrying out of a doorway and made her way across the playground. She beamed at me. 'How did it go? Looks like you've been having fun!'

'Miss Ghosh's class came out to do PE,' I began, but Mrs Drew had just spotted Martin Coggles.

'That's a nasty nose bleed you have there, Martin. Have some of the boys been a bit rough?'

'Id wad Gloria Bevindod,' Martin growled.

The head teacher threw back her head and laughed. 'Gloria Bevinson? A four-year-old giving a ten-year-old a big nose bleed like that? Don't be ridiculous! Come on then, everyone inside, fun and games over for today. I'm quite sure that our famous guests tomorrow are going to love your film, Jamie.'

Inwardly I groaned. Yeah. They were going to love my film about as much as you love a pie in the face. My dream of Krazy Kow had turned into my worst nightmare ever. Would it never end?

10 Krazy Kow's Last Battle

Scene One

[*Dark and jangly music. The Gobb-Yobb
theme tune*]

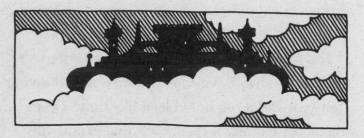

Castle Corruption floats high in the ice-bound air
above Antarctica. Gobb-Yobb Badmash lies upon his
black throne and soaks up the extra radiation that
comes pouring through the huge ozone hole.
Secretary Snirch hovers at his elbow, holding a fresh
bowl of worms.

'Is evewything weady for the final showdown with
that widiculous moo-cow, Snirch?'

'It is, Great Monster of Misery. There is a rubbish

heap in Switzerland that should provide a good theatre for the last act of this drama.'

Gobb-Yobb sits up, looking considerably displeased. 'A wubbish heap? You mean we aren't going to blow up a nuclear power station or weck a giant oil tanker? And why Switzerland? It's such a weeny-teeny little place. Nothing but snow and mountains and cuckoo clocks.'

'Exactly,' says Snirch smoothly. 'It is a place of mountains, many of them, and I have made an interesting discovery, Plague-Master.'

'Weally?' Gobb-Yobb smiles and nibbles on a particularly tasty (and wriggly) worm.

'There is a mountain that has been completely hollowed out. The Swiss have been using it for years as a place to hide their rubbish.'

'Aha! A mountain of wubbish!'

'Quite so,' smiles Snirch. 'But now the mountain is full, and all that rotting vegetation and stuff, and of course you know what methane smells like ...'

'Bad eggs! Pooo-eee! Wonderful!'

'Quite. So we start a little fire, the sort of accident that might so easily happen. The fire threatens to ignite the methane. It's a giant volcano waiting to erupt. An emergency call goes out ...'

'And Kwazy Kow comes zooming to the wescue.'

[Gobb-Yobb sings the Krazy Kow theme tune in his high voice: **'Dooooo-bee doodle-oo, diddle-iddle-eeee, diddly-dum-bee-dum-bee-dum, widdly-tiddly-deee'** *etc.]*

'And right on top of the mountain is our little chicken, ready and waiting.' Secretary Snirch folds his arms and waits.

Gobb-Yobb smiles. The more he thinks about this plan the better

Oh sweet, sweet wevenge!

he likes it. It will do away with his arch-enemy at last, but it also has a delicious twist: not only Krazy Kow but the humans too are going to die at the hands of their own rubbish. And in Switzerland! SWITZERLAND! Gobb-Yobb is almost beside himself with ecstasy.

'Don't you see? It's the home of the Swiss army penknife and Kwazy Kow's howwible, howwendous Swiss army udder! Oh sweet, sweet wevenge!' Gobb-Yobb Badmash, the Dark Contaminator, gazes blissfully at his assistant and sighs.

'Oh Snirch, I think I'm in heaven! I shall take the chicken myself.'

Scene Two

Krazy Kow is in the bath, singing. She is covered in foam and is trying to scrub her back with a long-handled scrubbing brush.

> '**Scrub-a-dub! Cow in the tub!**
> **There's an udder in the tubba;**
> **Rubba-dubba-dubba!**'

It isn't the best song Krazy Kow has written but she seems to be enjoying it.

Outside the bathroom door Gosforth heaves a sigh. She reckons she has been waiting outside for hours. She sits down and leans back against the wall. She twists her head and shouts through the keyhole.

'How much longer?'

'Would you rather the world is saved by a clean cow or a dirty one?' Krazy Kow shouts back. She juggles the soap, a bottle of shampoo and the nail brush and carries on singing.

'I am the shiny, shiniest cow,
doo-bee-doo-bee-doo;
My public want me shiny,
'cos I'm the Biggest Moo!
Moooooooo-ooooo!'

Bromley suddenly comes pounding up the stairs, three at a time.

'RED ALERT!' he yells. 'Telly's on red alert!'

Krazy Kow scrambles to her feet, which is very difficult when you're a cow and you're in a wet bath with slippery sides. 'DON'T PANIC!' she yells, 'I shall be there in a whizz!' She flings a towel around her body and almost falls down the stairs.

[Sound effect: clattering down stairs]

'At last,' moans Gosforth, sneaking into the bathroom and locking the door.

Scene Three

Downstairs the television is going bananas.

[Phwheep! Phweep! Phweep! Phweep!]

'This is the International Emergency, Help, Somebody Do Something Quickly Committee. There's a major fire at the world's biggest rubbish dump in Switzerland. It won't be much longer before an entire mountain of methane gas explodes, which will in turn send thousands of tons of burning rubbish flying through the air, which will in turn start fires across several countries, which will in turn set countless cities ablaze, which will in turn kill millions of innocent people, which will ...'

'OK ... I GET THE PICTURE!' yells Krazy Kow. 'There's yet another pollution disaster in the making. I'm on my way! To the bathroom and beyond!'

Scene Four

Krazy Kow races back upstairs [*clatter clatter clatter*] only to find the door locked. She hammers upon it [*bang bang bang*].

'YOU'RE TOO LATE,' shouts Gosforth. 'You've had your go. It's my turn now.'

'But Switzerland is about to go up in flames, and only I can save her!' cries Krazy Kow.

Let me in!

'Tough!'

'Don't you care about all those people out there?'

'Nope.'

'Don't you care that a million billion tons of rubbish will be spread across the globe?'

'Nope. I'm having a bath.'

[*Sound of splashing*]

Outside the bathroom door Krazy Kow sits down with a frown. 'Hmmm,' she mutters. 'Children are so

thoughtless these days. Ah! But of course! The
downstairs toilet! Why didn't I think of that before?'
  [Clatter clatter clatter]

Scene Five

The cow shoots downstairs and vanishes into the
smallest room. She pulls on her Krazy Kape, her
udderpants and diamanté mask. She brushes her
teeth and combs the chunky bit between her ears.
She slaps on some lipstick and she squeezes out
through the window. And with a whizz and a pat and
a supersonic bang she is on her way to Switzerland.

*['Like a rocket into the blue! She's black and
white – she's Krazy Moooo! Dooooo-bee
doodle-oo, diddle-iddle-eeee, diddly-dum-bee-
dum-bee-dum, widdly-tiddly-deee,' etc. (The
new No. 1 hit – the KK theme tune)]*

Scene Six

By the time Krazy Kow reaches the rubbish mountain, the fire has truly taken hold.

[Crackle crackle crackle]

A thousand water cannons are arranged in a great circle round the edges of the dump. Behind the

water cannons stand a million onlookers who can't resist coming to stare at the disaster that is about to blow them all up.

Swiss Army General Flombay gazes upon the roaring flames. 'She's gonna blow any second. It's a good thing you're here, Krazy Kow.'

'Oh, I try to help where I can. What bothers me, General, is that there seem to be too many of these pollution problems taking place around the world. I'm beginning to think that they may have been started deliberately.'

[Astonished music: **Pwannnngggggggggg!**]

A huge crowd turns and stares at the cow in disbelief and shouts in chorus. 'DELIBERATELY?!'

[Even more astonished:

Pwwwaaaaaannnnnnnnnggggggggg!!]

'But what kind of evil villain would do a thing like that?'

'Me!' cries a huge, slug-like figure, jumping out of the shadows. At least he would have jumped if he had legs, but he hasn't, so he doesn't. He sort of slippy-slides instead.

[Doom-beedoom-bee dumdumdumdum DAH!!!]

'And who are you?' demands Swiss Army General Flombay.

'I am Gobb-Yobb Badmash, the Dark Contaminator, Pwince of Pestilence and Plague Master.'

'And I am Krazy Kow, the Big Moo,' cries our hero. 'Take that!

But what's this? Gobb-Yobb doesn't bat an eyelid. 'It's no good standing there making silly noises, Kwazy Kow. I'm not fwightened of you!'

'Really? Well I shall soon change your mind, Flobb-Splobb.' Krazy Kow spins her udder menacingly, and fixes the criminal mastermind with a narrow-eyed glare.

'You are not the least bit tewwifying,' insists Gobb-Yobb.

'No? Then how about –
THIS!' Krazy Kow suddenly
sticks both hoofs in her
mouth and pulls a horrible
face, sticking out her big pink
tongue as far as she can and
shaking it violently.
Brrrrrrrrrrrrrrrrrrrr!

And still Gobb-Yobb doesn't budge. Instead he
calmly opens his cloak of darkness and pulls out
what looks like some kind of mechanical chicken.
'Do you know what this is, Kwazy Kow?'

[Peck peck peck, Cock-a-doodle-DOOOM!!]

Krazy Kow takes a step back, her eyes bulging.
She swallows hard. 'Surely it isn't …? It can't be.
No, not a …'

'… Yes, exactly. Kwazy
Kow, your last hour has
come. It is time for you
to meet NUCLEAR
WEACTOR CHICKEN!'
*[Dan-deran-dan-
DANNNNN!!!]*

11 In the Pink

I went to bed thinking: It's a new day tomorrow.
It will be a good day. I haven't had a good day for
ages, so it's about time. I'm going to meet Kooky
Savage and everything is going to be brilliant!

There was a loud, despairing wail from
downstairs. It was so awful that everyone
in the house rushed to see what it
was. Mum was standing in the
kitchen, speechless. She had
just opened the washing
machine and found all the
stuff that Cat and I
had bunged in there
for cleaning the day
before – remember all
the strawberry-stained
stuff?

It came out clean all right but it was no longer white. It was pink. All those mashed-up strawberries stained everything that went into the machine and turned the whole lot as pink as a strawberry milkshake.

And that included Matt's one and only football kit.

And the county football trial was the next day.

Big Bro was going to have to wear a stunningly pink football kit.

He was not a happy bunny.

'Can't you wash it again?' Matt pleaded.

'I could, but this kind of stain will never come out. I'm sorry.'

'I shall look totally stupid,' scowled Matt. (He would, too!)

'You'll be fine,' said Mum. (Did you know that parents lie to their own children?!) 'I'll give it a good ironing.'

'The county selectors won't be looking at your football kit,' Dad pointed out helpfully. 'They'll be watching you for your football skills.'

'I'm going to look so stupid,' Matt repeated.

Gemma came downstairs. I hadn't seen her smile since that little problem with Justin and the video, but now her face lit up. She patted Matt on his head and he shrunk away from her, as if  she was putting a jinx on him.

'That looks nice,' she said brightly. 'Getting in touch with your feminine side, are you?'

'Gemma!' hissed Mum. 'Do you have to?'

'Do I have to what? I said it looked nice.'

'Yeah, but that's not what you meant,' snapped Matt.

'How do you know?' Gemma and Big Bro eyeballed each other.

'Because it looks daft,' I ventured. They spun round and glared at me.

'Who asked you?' Big Bro spat out, while Gemma looked at me as if I was something unspeakably horrible. So, I thought, she's still not speaking to me.

'We've had enough from you,' Dad put in and now I found all four members of my own family lined up against me, scowling.

'We've got a busy day ahead tomorrow,' snapped Dad. 'And we can do without your help. Matt's got a very important trial for the county team. It's his big chance.'

I watched them fussing round Matt and I thought, OK, it's about time everyone knew my little secret.

'As it happens, I've got a busy day too,' I said. 'Dwight Trellis and Kooky Savage are coming to the school to see my film about Krazy Kow, and I'll just repeat that for you: MY film about Krazy Kow.'

Dad stopped in his tracks. 'Dwight Trellis? The United winger? Coming to see *you*?'

I nodded. Just for once I had actually managed to impress my dad.

Gemma shook her head as if she couldn't believe it either. 'Kooky Savage? The film star? The real Kooky? Coming to see *you*?'

I nodded again. At last Gemma had spoken to me! 'They're visiting the schools which have submitted the best ideas for that competition I told you about ages ago, when you weren't listening.' I watched their astonished faces. I was getting my first taste of fame, and I couldn't resist pushing it further. 'Kooky Savage thinks Krazy Kow would make a good film. She wants to be in it.'

(OK, so maybe I was beginning to exaggerate – but it was the look on their faces, you see. They

were SO surprised. I loved every minute of it, every second, every silly milli-second! I wanted it to go on and on until their eyeballs fell out of their heads with sheer amazement.)

I had to tell them exactly when all this was happening. Dad reckoned he was going to come up to the school to get Dwight's autograph. I said I could get it for him, but Dad wanted to see the great United winger with his own eyes.

'The football trials will be over by the afternoon,' said Dad. 'We can all come up to the school.'

Gemma said she wanted to see Kooky Savage. And as for Mum, she wanted to see both the stars turn out. At that point I forgot all about exaggerating things and Reality began to kick in. My whole family were going to turn up at the school so that they could see Dwight Trellis and Kooky Savage watching my film.

WHAT FILM?!?!?

So far all we had were a few shots of Krazy Kow being chased by Mashmen wearing bin liners, who were being chased in turn by what

looked like gnomes in knickers. The film footage
finished with Gloria Bevinson trying to stuff the
great cow superhero into the infants' toilets. It was
not exactly the sort of film that makes a
Hollywood blockbuster.

When Mum dropped Big Bro and me off at
school the next day neither of us was very happy.
Matt was in his pink football kit, and I was
wondering how on Earth I was going to impress
Kooky Savage. I wasn't bothered about Dwight
whassisname because he was a footballer, but
Kooky would have the sort of contacts I needed.
She would know film directors, producers, other
film stars. She could be really useful to me, so I
had to make a deep impression.

I winkled out Cat and told her everything that
was going through my head. 'It's going to be a
disaster,' I moaned. 'Everyone will think it's
rubbish, and they'll be right.'

'It's going to be OK.'

I gave a hollow laugh. 'Oh, yeah, like Kooky
Savage is going to be so impressed by a
pantomime cow that can't act, and little kids

dressed up in bin liners. I'm going to tell Mrs Drew to stop filming and dump the lot. Then I can explain to Kooky Savage how it would have been if it had been done as a cartoon.'

'But you can't just throw away everything you've done already,' Cat wailed.

'Listen, if a great film director shoots some bad stuff he doesn't show it to the public, he bins it, right?'

Cat was silent for a while. She shook her head. 'How can you do that? How can you destroy the best thing you ever invented?' Eventually she lifted her head and gave me such a look it was as if someone had switched off all the lights inside her. I hadn't realized until that moment how much energy and enthusiasm she had been passing on to me. I didn't realize until I switched it off.

I shrugged. 'The whole project is falling to bits.'

'Seems like running away to me.'

'Krazy Kow can't even waddle with those two idiots inside her.'

'I don't mean Krazy Kow. You're the one that's running away. Things get tough, and you run away. I thought you wanted to be famous.'

'So?' Another shrug.

'It's your big chance, Jamie. At least have a go at it. If you don't have a go you've got no chance of success. At least try.'

'It's too late,' I muttered. 'It's finished. I'm finished. We're all finished.'

Cat got to her feet and looked down at me. 'I always thought I was the smallest person in our class. I was wrong. It's you.' She turned on her heel and walked off, leaving me with my eyes fixed on her back.

I was so confused. I'd never really thought of Cat as a friend. I don't think I'd thought of her as anything really, but now, all of a sudden, I desperately didn't want her to go. I hurled myself after her and caught up with her, panting.

'OK, tell me, what do we do?'

'You're the director,' she said simply. 'Give directions.'

I began to smile. Of course! This whole thing had been going wrong because we had been trying to film Krazy Kow the way other people wanted it, and in particular the way Mrs Drew wanted it. It was time to do it my way. It was too late to start making a cartoon, but maybe there was still enough time to film a really good episode with the pantomime cow. I just had to make sure that only the actors in the film knew what we were planning.

'We need loads of action,' I said.

'And explosions!' shouted Cat, and all her lights came back on.

'We can use the zip wire on the Air Cadets' training ground so that it looks like Krazy Kow is really flying through the air ...'

'... Yeah, and she can be firing her Swiss army udder ...'

'... Yeah, and we can have gallons of fake blood everywhere ...'

'... And horrible screams!' cried Cat. We

grabbed each other and did a little dance.

'It's going to be AWESOME!' we chorused.

There was a stifled giggle from near by and I looked up to see Rebecca watching us. Tom Hardy was standing behind her.

'Look, Tom, two little love birds,' Rebecca teased. He sniggered.

Cat turned a deep red and stared at her feet. 'Just ignore them,' she whispered through gritted teeth, but for once I didn't want to ignore them. I slipped one arm round Cat's shoulder, pulled her closer and kissed her.

(ONLY ON THE CHEEK! I'M NOT MAD!)

Cat looked up at me with an enormous smile, while Rebecca and Tom's mouths dropped open and all their brains fell out. They were speechless!

It felt like – you know what it felt like? – it was as if I had just walked up to a two-headed dragon and chopped off both heads with a single blow – swisssssh! It was dead and gone. For ever.

Cat and I turned and walked away from them. I still had my arm round her. Things were going to be OK after all.

12 Stars and Stuff

And then again, maybe not.

It was not difficult to persuade the cast of the film to take part in the new idea. In fact they thought it was brilliant, and their enthusiasm was catching. I began to feel more and more that we were going to be successful after all. I could almost smell that Oscar for Best Director, and maybe another one for Best Screenplay. I got everyone into a huddle and we talked things through.

'We must keep Mrs Drew out of the way so that she doesn't interfere and spoil everything. We also need a Special Effects Department. We need blood and we need weapons that can be fired through Krazy Kow's udder.'

'Can we have a crashing car somersaulting across the playground and bursting into flames?' This query came from Kingston. He's got a good imagination, but he gets a bit unreal sometimes.

'I don't think so, Kingston.'

'Huh.'

'How are we going to keep Mrs Drew out of the way?' asked Wayne Ribble.

'Good question. You can be in charge of that one, Wayne.' (I thought: Nice one, Jamie, pass the problem back to the person who thought of it!)

'Me?' Wayne looked worried.

'Yeah, you and Kingston.' Now Wayne looked even more worried, but Kingston was already on his feet.

'Great! We can tie her up. Yeah, we can tie her up an' stick a bomb on her head. Come on, Wayne!'

That got those two out of the way.

Carl had turned white. 'He doesn't really mean that, does he?'

I burst out laughing. 'Don't be stupid! You know what Kingston's like. Anyhow, Wayne will keep him in order. OK, so what's next?'

Cat had some suggestions. 'I've been thinking about blood. In films they use fake blood, yeah? That's easy. We can make up some sloppy red paint. But the fake blood is usually put in capsules or something. How do we do that?'

I grinned at everyone. 'We fill balloons with the fake blood and stuff them up our clothes, and when we burst them the blood will come oozing out.'

The others looked at me and Cat as if we were superstars. (And, of course, we were! Well, almost.)

'Weapons?' This came from Carl.

'Leave that to me,' I said. I was reckoning on phoning Mum at home and getting her to bring my ping-pong gun and water cannon to school. Carl was looking mystified.

'What I can't see is this: Martin and me are inside Krazy Kow, right? If we slide down the zip wire, how are we going to grip the runner handles? Our hands are inside the costume.'

'Then you'll have to stick your hands out to hold on,' I said.

'Won't that look odd?'

'Not if I film it from the right angle. That's what they do when they're making a film in Hollywood. You film it from an angle that doesn't show what's actually making it work – like when cars flip over. They use a metal prong that springs up under the car and flips it. But they don't film the metal prong – they just film the car itself, flying through the air.'

Carl looked at me happily and nodded. I went on.

'The only thing is that there's only one runner handle for the wire. That means you'll both have to hang on to it.'

Martin had been frowning hard for the last five minutes. He was obviously brooding on something. 'So I have to hang on to the runner handle with two hands and I have to fire the guns through my Swiss army udder with my other two hands?'

'What other two hands?' demanded Carl crossly. 'You haven't got four hands.'

'Exactly,' Martin agreed.

The three of us gazed at each other. Martin  had a point, and it was an awkward one. Cat came to the rescue and she asked Carl if he thought he was strong enough to hang on for two people?

'Yeah, I think so. It won't take long for us to reach the ground.'

'OK, then suppose we put a rope harness round Martin, and tie the rope round Carl's trouser belt. Martin can hang there inside, leaving both hands free to fire the udder guns.'

It was such a good solution that we just sat

there, smiling at each other. We were going to
make this thing work!

'Kooky Savage is really going to wish she was
in our film,' I grinned.

By the time the lunch-hour arrived the whole
school was in a state of high excitement.
Everyone was awaiting the arrival of the two
superstars. In the meantime the Special Effects
Department had managed to knock up a tub full
of fake blood, made with crimson powder paint
and water. The weapons had arrived too. The
school secretary was slightly surprised when Mum
turned up with a delivery of water cannons and
ping-pong bazookas, but when Mum said it was
for the film the secretary assumed that it was Mrs
Drew who had asked for them.

Everything was set. The guests arrived.

I never expected Dwight Trellis to be so tall.
When you watched a United game on telly you
could see him whizzing about the place, leaping
into the air, heading the ball and so on, but the
TV didn't give any real idea of his size. He must

have been over two metres. He towered above everyone.

There were kids all round him, clamouring for his autograph. Dwight stood there with a huge smile, merrily signing away and chatting to them all.

There was another seething mass of kids surrounding Kooky Savage. Now that I could see her close up I realized that she was truly beautiful. She was Glamour On Legs.

'I can't breathe,' she kept saying. 'Give me a bit of space, will you? I neeeeed SPACE!' Yet another piece of paper was thrust under her nose. 'What's

that – toilet paper? I can't sign a teeny bit of scrumpled rubbish like that.' Kooky suddenly screeched at the top of her voice. 'PROPER AUTOGRAPH BOOKS ONLY! I REFUSE TO SIGN DIDDLY SCRAPS OF PAPER.'

A hundred children groaned. 'Please, Miss Savage, we haven't got proper autograph books. We've got clean paper, look.'

Kooky Savage stood firm, folding her arms across her chest. 'Autograph books only.'

One by one the children drifted away from Kooky and joined the throng round Dwight Trellis instead. He was still going great guns, scribbling his name across anything that moved.

'He signed the plaster on my broken arm,' said one kid.

'So? He's done my shirt,' said another.

'He signed my HEAD!' cried Wayne Ribble, and it was true. Wayne had recently had one of those Everything Must Go haircuts that had left him bald and shiny. Now he had Dwight Trellis written across his skull.

Mrs Drew and the teaching staff appeared and they began to impose some sense of order on everything. The head teacher called me over and introduced me to Kooky Savage.

'Hell's bells, I've never seen so many kids,' muttered Kooky, and Mrs Drew gave the film star a sharp look.

'It's a school,' she said.

'Never seen so many,' repeated Kooky, almost as if she was frightened.

Mrs Drew pushed me forward. 'This is Jamie Frink. Jamie is the one who invented Krazy Kow and all the other characters.'

'I'm very pleased to meet you,' I began, holding out my hand.

Kooky Savage kept her arms folded. She didn't even look at me, but gazed round behind her. 'Is there any food? My agent said there'd be food.'

Mrs Drew kept smiling. 'Jamie also had the idea of making a film instead of writing an ordinary story or an essay. It was clever of him, don't you think?'

'It wasn't just my idea,' I said. 'My friend Cat

helped me.' I smiled across at Cat and beckoned to her to come and join us. Cat hurried over, looking rather red with embarrassment, as usual. 'She's a great fan of yours,' I added.

'Cat?' Kooky Savage looked mildly astonished. 'What kind of a name is that?'

Cat's face fell. She couldn't think what to say.

The film star laughed. 'What's the matter? Cat got your tongue?' Kooky screamed with laughter and looked at each one of us to make sure we all realized how clever and funny she was being.

Mrs Drew smiled back at the film star. 'Where did you get your name from, Kooky?'

And that was when I saw my first real superhero. That was when Mrs Drew suddenly turned into Fearless Headmistress-Woman, Super-Wonder-Creature!

Kooky Savage snapped a glare on Mrs Drew. 'What?' she asked, icily.

'You were saying that Cat was an odd name, and it made me wonder how you got to be called Kooky.  As you can imagine we come across all sorts of names in a school – but we've never had a Kooky.'

Cat had her teeth and lips clenched together firmly. So did I. We were desperately trying not to laugh. Luckily we were saved at that moment by the arrival of Matt and Tom, along with Gemma and my parents.

Dad bellowed across the playground. 'Dwight! I'm your biggest fan!'

Dwight Trellis gazed across at my idiotic father, running across the playground, waving his arms like some great big child.

'You can't be my biggest fan,' Dwight shouted back easily. 'I've got fans four times as big as you!' They both fell about laughing, while Dad shoved some paper into the winger's hand, for signing.

Gemma had come up, rather shyly, to see Kooky Savage.

'This is my big sister,' I said. Gemma gave a curtsy, as if Kooky were the Queen, and like me she held out a hand. Kooky ignored it.

'You're bigger than the others,' she observed.

'I'm older,' said Gemma, as if that weren't obvious anyhow.

'Why are you still at this school then? Are you thick?' The film star looked around once more. 'My agent said there'd be some food.'

Gemma was stunned. Her eyes had that look in them, the kind of hopeless, blank stare that you

see on the faces of people whose dreams have just been wiped out by a few casual words.

Mrs Drew bustled to the rescue once again. 'Let's move over to the film set. That is after all what you have come for – to see some of the filming take place. I'm sure you are going to enjoy it.'

As they went I noticed a pink figure hanging around the back of the crowd surrounding Dwight Trellis. It was Big Bro. I'd been so busy I had completely forgotten about the football trial. I groaned inwardly. He was going to be so big-headed now. He was going to be insufferable. I went over to him.

'How did it go?' I asked.

'How do you think it went? I was the only pink footballer there. I didn't make the team. Now shove off.'

13 The Greatest Film Ever

'You didn't make the team?'

'Look at my poxy football kit! Are you surprised?'

'What about Tom Hardy? Did he get picked?'

Matt grimly shook his head. I asked Big Bro if Tom had been wearing a pink football kit too.

'Of course he wasn't! I was the only one!' Matt thundered back at me, but I held my ground.

'You always said Tom was better than you,' I pointed out. 'And if Tom didn't get chosen and he wasn't wearing a pink kit, then the pink kit had nothing to do with it – that's all I'm trying to say.'

Matt fell silent, but I could tell he was still seething so I left him to it. There was nothing more I could do there. Anyhow, I was supposed to be over at the training ground by now, shooting the film.

I raced back across the playground to join Mrs Drew and the VIP party as they headed for the filming area. The secretary came bustling out of the school, looking very flustered. It seemed as if there had been some kind of emergency phone call. Mrs Drew would have to go and deal with it.

'I'm so sorry to leave you all,' Mrs Drew apologized. 'I'm sure the children will look after you. Jamie will explain what we're doing and I shall get back as quickly as possible.'

This was obviously part of Wayne and Kingston's plan to get the head teacher out of the way. My heart lifted. Everything was going just right. I walked along between our two visiting superstars, wondering if some of their fame would fall off them and land on me.

'You wrote this film, did you?' asked Dwight.

'Yes. The whole thing was my idea.'

The footballer pursed his lips thoughtfully. 'I wish I could write. I'd love to write.'

'Why don't you?' I asked.

'Me? I'm a footballer, me.'

'That shouldn't stop you writing,' I said. There was a snort from Kooky. 'Anyone can write. That's what I think, anyhow. Just let your imagination roll, like a film going on inside your head.'

Dwight frowned. 'Yeah. Maybe you're right. I should have a go.' He paused and looked down at me from his great height. 'Thanks,' he added.

Thanks! Dwight Trellis, the United's ace winger had just said 'thanks' to me! There was another snort from beside me.

'Be surprised if he can write his own name,' muttered Kooky under her breath, obviously thinking that nobody could hear.

Cat and the others were waiting impatiently beneath the zip wire. Carl and Martin had already climbed the big oak tree and were on the platform. They stood there inside the cow costume, ready to start.

'Have you got the weapons?' I shouted up.

There was a muffled reply from inside which I took to mean a 'yes'.

'Does everybody know what to do?' Nods all round. 'In that case let's do it! Here come Dwight and Kooky. Cat, you take them over to the chairs and sit them down, while I set the camera. Everybody else, wait for my command.'

Cat led the protesting actress to her seat. 'Where's the cushion?' she demanded.

'They don't have cushions,' Cat told her.

Kooky eyed Cat suspiciously. 'I've seen you before somewhere. Aren't you called Dog, or something?'

Cat ignored her and showed Dwight to his chair. Behind the stars the teachers, my parents and Gemma settled into their seats.

The big footballer beamed at everybody. 'This

looks good. I've never seen a film being made before.'

'Have you got a cushion?' Kooky asked him and he shook his head. 'No cushions,' muttered Kooky. 'No food. It's a disgrace.'

I could hear everything the film star was saying, but I tried to ignore her and concentrate on the film. This was make or break time. It had to be really good, and I was sure it was going to be a billion times better than anything we had filmed before.

I shouted to the cast. 'Are the Mashmen ready?'

'Ready!'

'Krazy Kow?'

'NO!' yelled Carl. 'Martin's cut his arm on a branch. He can't do it.'

Why is it always like this? Why is it that things always go wrong at the very worst moment? My brain struggled desperately to think of a solution. I felt Cat push past me.

'I'll do it,' she muttered, and before I could say anything she was halfway up the tree to join Carl.

She grinned down, gave me a wave and a moment later she vanished inside the back half of the cow.

'OK,' I roared. 'Action!'

Inside the cow Cat swung from Carl's waist. Carl reached up, gripped the runner handles and launched himself from the platform. The roller wheels hummed and picked up speed. At first Krazy Kow seemed to wobble, but then down she came, looking utterly glorious and fabulous, shining in the bright sunlight.

Martin let off a burst of fast tempo music from the sound system. Then the Mashmen appeared, running across the grass towards Krazy Kow, their black bin-bag capes flying behind them as they hurled themselves into battle.

Cat got to work with the ping-pong bazooka.
All at once Krazy Kow's udder had something
sticking out of it.

'I am the Big Moo!' roared Carl,
while Cat let rip and ping-
pong balls went whizz-
pip in every direction.
Some of the Mashmen
gave blood-curdling yells and fell over
as if they'd been hit, bursting their balloons
and squirting fake blood everywhere. Cat
swapped to the water cannon and suddenly a
steady jet of ice-cold water was sprayed
everywhere.

SPLAT!!

It hit Dwight on the chest and he toppled
backwards, so that the whole of the row behind
got plastered – Mum, Dad,
Gemma and all the teachers.

SPLOPP-A-DOPP!!

It spattered across
Kooky's face. She
was so shocked that

she stood up,
slipped on the wet
grass beneath her
feet and sat down
again.

Unfortunately her
chair was no longer
there and she ended up on her backside in the
mud. She struggled to get back to her feet and
was met with a hail of ping-pong balls.

Ping-poppa ping-ping-pong pippa poppa ping!

At this point Krazy Kow suddenly gave a
dreadful cry and split in half. Carl's trouser belt
(and his trousers!) had given way under the strain
and Cat fell to the ground, a short distance below.

Meanwhile Carl, wearing
a cow's head on his top
half and his underpants on
the bottom, carried on
merrily swinging down the
zip wire until he finally came
to rest on the ground. He
immediately set about

splashing back through the pools of fake blood in his bare legs, to where Cat was still firing ping-pong balls into the air. Carl grabbed his trousers and tried to put them back on, only to fall into yet another pool of blood.

This last bit of the action had been watched in almost silent horror by everyone except Kooky Savage, who was still struggling to rescue herself from the mud and a million ping-pong balls. Every time she attempted to raise herself a leg or an arm would suddenly slip from beneath her and she'd be flat on her front, or back, or side, or bottom.

And then Dwight Trellis started laughing. He stood there like a happy giant, chuckling at everything around him. He was in stitches. He bent double, and his laughter rang out across the training ground.

Kooky Savage at last managed to get to her feet. She was plastered with mud, and she promptly made matters worse by trying to brush the worst away.

'WHERE IS THE HEAD TEACHER?' she screeched. 'My lawyer is going to hear about this! Fetch me the head teacher at once!'

Kooky began to stride back to the school. Cat and I hurried after her, with Cat trailing behind, trying to free herself from the remains of the KK's back half.

'It wasn't meant to be like that,' I tried to say.

'I have never been so insulted!'

'Things got a bit out of hand,' I mumbled.

'A BIT OUT OF HAND! THEY WERE OFF THIS PLANET!' screamed the actress. 'And as for you,' she squawked, turning on Cat. 'You fired that thing at me deliberately!'

'My hair got in my eyes,' said Cat, with a completely straight face. (Her hair doesn't even reach her eyebrows, let alone her eyes.)

By this time we had reached the school buildings and Kooky made straight for Mrs Drew's office, her high heels making a machine-gun racket on the wooden floor. Cat and I trailed miserably behind.

Kooky didn't bother to knock. She burst through the door, still shouting, and instantly fell silent. Sitting behind her desk, tied to her chair, was Mrs Drew. Strapped to Mrs Drew's head was a packet with red writing on it in big felt tip pen. It said:

BoM!

Sitting on the floor next to Mrs Drew was the school secretary, also tied up. And lounging on a chair watching them, with his feet up on the desk, a big grin on his face and chewing a pencil like a cigar, was Kingston.

'How's it going?' he asked cheerfully.

13 ½ Time to Tidy Up Loose Ends

There was an awful lot of shouting (from Kooky Savage) and even more rushing about (from Cat and me as we untied Mrs Drew and the secretary) and some more shouting (from Kooky again) and then Mrs Drew asked for an explanation.

So I told her everything. Her face began to take on that expression that warns you that things are about to turn into a ton of bricks and fall on you, but halfway through all this Dwight Trellis, the front half of a pantomime cow and a bedraggled crowd of bloodstained onlookers arrived from the filming.

'It was fantastic, Mrs Drew,' enthused the United winger. 'The best thing I have seen for ages. I know it all went wrong but at least they tried, and I want to tell you something. When I was at school we were never allowed to even think

about doing something as ambitious as this
filming idea of yours. I reckon you're running a
top team here, with top kids, judging by what I've
seen today. You should all be proud of yourselves.'

Beside him, Kooky was desperately trying to
draw breath. She was so shocked at what she was
hearing she could not even bring herself to speak
at first. But she eventually found her tongue, and
then she began. She went on and on, her voice
getting louder and louder and higher and higher,
until she was squeaking away like some demented
rat, listing one complaint after another.

Dwight waited until the film star had finished
and then told her that she was completely missing
the point.

'Everything you've complained about has been about you,' he said. 'It's all YOU, isn't it? That's all you think about. We've come here to judge a competition which is about saving this planet from people like you, people who only think about themselves. You are the most wretchedly thoughtless person I have ever met. Every one of these children here is worth a hundred of you! Even him!' (Here Dwight pointed at Kingston and gave him a huge wink.)

Kooky stared at the footballer, gobsmacked. 'You don't like me, do you?'

'You're dead right there,' agreed Dwight. 'And I don't suppose anyone else does either.'

Kooky slumped into a chair and burst into tears. Great, gulping sobs filled the head's office. The rest of us quietly slipped out and closed the door on her. Only Rebecca stayed behind.

(Remember her? She now seemed like someone from a distant dream, way back in my past.) Rebecca stayed with Kooky, crouching at the film star's feet and patting her knees.

'I think you're wonderful,' Rebecca crooned. 'I'm going to be just like you.'

I'll cut out most of what happened after that, but as you can probably imagine, there was a lot of sorting out to do. Mrs Drew came up trumps. She said she understood what I was trying to do and that although she could not say that what Kingston had done was the right thing, she applauded his enthusiasm. (And that's a lot more than I would have done if he'd tied me up and strapped a pretend bomb to my head. I would have killed him!)

Of course, it was the end of all the filming and the project. We never did get it finished and we never won the competition. But I discovered all sorts of things, such as:

1. Sometimes you meet people who you don't

expect to be nice, but they are, like Dwight Trellis.

2. And sometimes people can look nice, but they aren't. (No names!)

3. And then there are other people, Cat for example, who doesn't look like anything much (except perhaps a small, half asleep, slightly scruffy moggy) but are really nice inside, and the totally weird thing is that when you realize how nice someone is inside, they begin to look beautiful on the outside after all.

A couple of days after the film disaster I got a package through the post. The label on the outside said it was from Awesome Film Productions, Hollywood. Was it the contract? I could hardly bring myself to open it, but I did. I pulled out a thick sheaf of paper and recognized it at once.

It was my film script. They were returning it. The letter they included simply said that they didn't want it and it finished with:

We wish you success in the future, but please don't bother to send us anything more until you're grown up.

When I read that last sentence in their letter I felt as if all along I'd been playing in a pink football kit. It's made me think a lot about Big Bro. I want to tell him I know how he feels about failing. Do you think I'm strong enough? Shall I tell him? Hmmm, maybe.

Of course Awesome Productions are probably the most stupid people in the whole world. Can't they see how good Krazy Kow is? I don't know how long I sat there reading their letter, over and over again, but it was the last straw. There didn't seem much point in going on.

Still, you're probably wondering how KK is going to escape from Gobb-Yobb Badmash and Nuclear Reactor Chicken, so read on!

The End. Krazy Kow's Last Battle

The Final Scene

Krazy Kow stares in horror at Nuclear Reactor
Chicken. 'How did you know my secret?' she asks in
a horrified whisper.

'I'm afwaid Bwomley Spottiswood is not as loyal
as he appears to be,' smiles Gobb-Yobb. 'A little
bwibewy – it didn't take much, and your secwet was
ours.'

'But if you explode that chicken it will not only
destroy me, but it will kill us all. You will set off a
chain reaction that will destroy the whole planet.'

[Horrified gasp from crowd: **'Oh!'** *]*

'I know,' said Gobb-Yobb.

'It will kill you too,' Krazy Kow points out.

'I know,' says Gobb-Yobb. 'That shows you just how evil I can be. Short-sighted, but evil.'

Secretary Snirch presses himself forward. 'Excuse me. I didn't know.'

'Too late now,' Gobb-Yobb cries. 'Say your pwayers, Kwazy Kow,'

Krazy Kow turns to the huddled onlookers. 'Listen up, everyone,' she moos. 'This is what I tell you: I am the Big ...'

BANG!

And they all died.

Oh dear.

What a pity.

The End

So there you are. That was the end of Krazy
Kow. She was a good idea while she lasted, but it's
time to move on to better things. You see, I've had
this amazingly brilliant idea for a film! It's going
to be fantastic – a million times better than Krazy
Kow. Cat and I are working on it together. (Cat
says we can use her dad's camera.)

It's all about a terrifying race of supermodels
who come from another planet (called Kookyville)
and the world can only be saved by a superhero
called Dangergoat and his sidekick Atomic
Elephant. I'm going to call it:

INVASION OF THE MONSTERMODELS

It's going to make me famous. People will
recognize me in the street and they'll say: 'Wow!
There goes Jamie Frink, the film director and
multimillionaire. I can't believe I've met Jamie
Frink. Can I have your autograph?'

And I'll say: 'Sure, have three. And if you ask
nicely I'm sure my friend Cat here will give you

hers too. And we don't mind doing them on
diddly bits of scrumpled paper, either.'

I haven't given up at all.

I am going to be a great film director.

Just you wait and see.

Ask Jeremy

Of all the books you have written, which one is your favourite?

I loved writing both **KRAZY KOW SAVES THE WORLD – WELL, ALMOST** and **STUFF**, my first book for teenagers. Both these made me laugh out loud while I was writing and I was pleased with the overall result in each case. I also love writing the stories about Nicholas and his daft family – **MY DAD**, **MY MUM**, **MY BROTHER** and so on.

If you couldn't be a writer what would you be?

Well, I'd be pretty fed up for a start, because writing was the one thing I knew I wanted to do from the age of nine onward. But if I DID have to do something else, I would love to be either an accomplished pianist or an artist of some sort. Music and art have played a big part in my whole life and I would love to be involved in them in some way.

What's the best thing about writing stories?

Oh dear – so many things to say here! Getting paid for making things up is pretty high on the list! It's also something you do on your own, inside your own head – nobody can interfere with that. The only boss you have is yourself. And you are creating something that nobody else has made before you. I also love making my readers laugh and want to read more and more.

Did you ever have a nightmare teacher? (And who was your best ever?)

My nightmare at primary school was Mrs Chappell, long since dead. I knew her secret – she was not actually human. She was a Tyrannosaurus rex in disguise. She taught me for two years when I was in Y5 and Y6, and we didn't like each other at all. My best ever was when I was in Y3 and Y4. Her name was Miss Cox, and she was the one who first encouraged me to write stories. She was brilliant. Sadly, she is long dead too.

When you were a kid you used to play kiss-chase. Did you always do the chasing or did anyone ever chase you?!

I usually did the chasing, but when I got chased, I didn't bother to run very fast! Maybe I shouldn't admit to that! We didn't play kiss-chase at school – it was usually played during holidays. If we had tried playing it at school we would have been in serious trouble. Mind you, I seemed to spend most of my time in trouble of one sort or another, so maybe it wouldn't have mattered that much.

14½ Things You Didn't Know About

Jeremy Strong

★ ★ ★ ★ ★ ★ ★ ★ ★ ★ ★ ★ ★ ★ ★ ★ ★

1. He loves eating liquorice.

2. He used to like diving. He once dived from the high board and his trunks came off!

3. He used to play electric violin in a rock band called **THE INEDIBLE CHEESE SANDWICH**.

4. He got a 100-metre swimming certificate when he couldn't even swim.

5. When he was five, he sat on a heater and burnt his bottom.

6. Jeremy used to look after a dog that kept eating his underpants. (No – NOT while he was wearing them!)

7. When he was five, he left a basin tap running with the plug in and flooded the bathroom.

8. He can make his ears waggle.

9. He has visited over a thousand schools.

10. He once scored minus ten in an exam! That's ten less than nothing!

11. His hair has gone grey, but his mind hasn't.

12. He'd like to have a pet tiger.

13. He'd like to learn the piano.

14. He has dreadful handwriting.

And a half . . . His favourite hobby is sleeping. He's very good at it.

This is the first story about my crazy family. We're not all crazy of course – it's Dad mostly. I mean, who would think of bringing home an alligator as a pet? It got into our next-door neighbour's garden and ate all the fish from his pond. It even got into his car! That gave him quite a surprise, I can tell you! He was not very happy about it. Mum says Crunchbag will have to go, but Dad and I quite like him, even if his teeth are rather big and sharp.

LAUGH YOUR SOCKS OFF WITH

MY DAD'S GOT AN ALLIGATOR!

Available Now!

* * * * * * * * * * * * * * * * * * * *

Big problems in my family – we're running out of money fast. Dad reckons we should start up our own mini-farm. But the yoghurt we made exploded, and the goat needed an aromatherapy massage!

   That's the sort of daft thing that happens in my family. And then my baby bro, Cheese (yes – I know Cheese is a very odd name for a baby!), was spotted on national television showing off his bottom!

LAUGH YOUR SOCKS OFF WITH

MY BROTHER'S FAMOUS BOTTOM

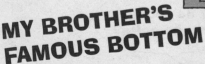

Available Now!

Psssst!

Look what we overheard . . .
What you really think about

Jeremy Strong . . .

Your mind is a basketful of ideas . . .

The pages really come to life

Your brain must always be on to have so many ideas

My pals just want to say that your books rule

We adore your books because they're hysterical!

Why do you wear strange belts?